DREAM DOCTOR

'*He's adorable!*' Having heard so much about Dr Mike Gregson, Nurse Susan Bradshaw looks forward to meeting him when she joins his emergency drought relief team in West Africa. But surely there's been some mistake? For no one could call the aggressive Dr Gregson who demolishes her on her first day at Kyruba Hospital *adorable*!

DREAM DOCTOR

BY
MARGARET BARKER

MILLS & BOON LIMITED
15–16 BROOK'S MEWS
LONDON W1A 1DR

First published in Great Britain 1985 by Mills & Boon Limited

© Margaret Barker 1985

Australian copyright 1985 Philippine copyright 1985

ISBN 0 263 75128 7

Set in 11½ on 12½ pt Linotron Times
03–0985–42,500

Photoset by Rowland Phototypesetting Ltd Bury St Edmunds, Suffolk Made and printed in Great Britain by Richard Clay (The Chaucer Press) Ltd Bungay, Suffolk

CHAPTER ONE

THE HOT tropical sun beat mercilessly down on the hospital compound as Susan ladled out the sticky breakfast food into the brightly-coloured tin bowl held out by an emaciated brown hand. Was it really only yesterday that she had flown in from London? It seemed light-years away.

This was not how Susan had imagined Matala from Kate's letters. Her best friend from PTS days in their London teaching hospital had always written in glowing terms about the work at Kyruba Hospital. Perhaps Kate's descriptions had been coloured by the fact that she was deeply in love with her husband, Dr Richard Brooks, Medical Consultant at Kyruba, and apparently living an idyllic life at the beautiful Ogiwa House outside the town. Certainly Susan had never imagined that on her first morning at Kyruba she would be standing in the sun dispensing stodgy-looking food.

She looked into the gaunt, care-worn face of the woman holding the bowl and smiled. A brief twitching of the woman's lips indicated that she had noticed Susan's friendliness, but she was much too intent on getting away to a quiet corner where she could eat her food, before suckling the tiny baby strapped to her back.

Susan sighed as she watched her shuffle away. Probably even younger than me, she thought, although, at twenty-three, Susan looked a generation younger than the famine-stricken young mother. She dipped the tin ladle deep into the life-giving grain mixture and served another portion into the next outstretched bowl. The same air of desperation surrounded this young mother. Susan's lively blue eyes looked into the woman's dull brown ones and she felt a deep sense of pity. Yes, in spite of everything, she was glad that she had come out to Africa to help to do something about the emergency situation created by the drought.

A small child standing by his mother's side was holding out his bowl. Susan patted his head gently as she gave him his portion.

'Nurse!' The command was brusque and imperious.

Susan turned in alarm to see who had issued it. The tall, arrogant figure of a man in a white coat was hovering behind her. He was standing in a direct line with the rays of the sun, and Susan had to shield her eyes to see him. His piercing blue eyes looked angry and impatient.

'Well, what are you going to do about him, Nurse?' he thundered. His sun-tanned skin was heightened with emotion as he gazed down at the hapless Susan.

'Do? About what?' she faltered.

'About the child, you incompetent girl,' he said menacingly. 'Surely you can see there must be something wrong by the way he's holding one hand behind his back?'

Susan turned to look at the small boy, who was looking bewildered by this sudden focus of attention. As the doctor leaned towards the child, his supercilious manner changed completely.

'Show me your hand, sonny,' he said gently, and then repeated his request in the soft, undulating language of the Kulani tribe. The boy looked up at his mother, who nodded imperceptibly. Slowly and reluctantly, the child held out the hand which had been behind his back.

Susan gasped when she saw it. The skin had been burned away from the palm, revealing a large open wound.

'As I thought,' muttered the doctor under his breath. 'Another burns case.' He spoke rapidly to the mother, who appeared immediately to be on the defensive.

'Nurse Hamlin,' he called, and the other staff nurse on duty came hurrying up, smoothing her starched white uniform and patting her pert little cap into place on the top of her auburn curls.

'Yes, Dr Gregson,' she said breathlessly.

'Second degree burns, Nurse,' he told her hurriedly. 'The usual treatment, please . . . I'll be along shortly, when I've finished supervising here.' His tone was ominous as he finished the sentence, in direct contrast to his gentle manner with the patient.

'Of course, Doctor.' Nurse Hamlin flashed him a bright smile which lit up the whole of her face, from the distinctive high cheekbones to the freckles on her nose. 'Come along, little man.' She lifted the child, still clinging firmly to his food bowl, into her arms and started to move away. As she did so she turned and gave Susan a sly wink.

'Don't worry, Susan,' she whispered. 'He's really rather adorable . . .'

Dr Gregson looked across enquiringly at the two nurses and Monica Hamlin hurried away with her small patient, followed by the anxious mother.

Susan was still smarting at the indignity of having been called incompetent but, like a true professional, she continued her important task without any hint of her inward annoyance.

'Is this your first day here, Nurse?' Dr Gregson asked quietly, as he watched her serve another portion of food.

'Yes, Doctor,' Susan said, concentrating all her attention on the mother and baby in front of her.

'One of the things you must remember,' he continued relentlessly, 'is that you are here not only to give out food, but also to observe any potential health problems. The morning food station is often our only contact with the refugees.'

'Yes, I see, Doctor,' Susan said, smoothly. 'I hadn't noticed the child's hand because it was behind his back. I'll try to . . .'

'Exactly, Nurse,' he interrupted. 'The child was holding the hand behind his back because he was afraid we should see it. The Kulani tribe are still very suspicious of the white man's medicine. They have come here from a very primitive territory in the north of Matala, and it will take them some time to adjust.'

It will take me some time to adjust too, thought Susan, but she did not voice her thoughts. Instead she raised her head and looked bravely into the piercing blue eyes as she said, 'Tell me, Doctor, what exactly is this concoction I'm serving?'

'Concoction!' he exploded, and Susan's gaze shifted uneasily. 'It's a well-balanced, nourishing, totally necessary foodstuff. The natives call it *gari*, because that's their predominant food, but we've added high-protein grain to it. As you can see, our main problem is malnutrition.'

He waved his arm in the direction of the long, straggling line of emaciated, dark-skinned women and children.

'Every morning it's the same,' he continued. 'They queue up for their rations, and then later in the day they try to cook something for themselves over their open fires out there in the refugee camp. That's when the burns start.'

'Thank you, Doctor,' Susan said quietly. 'I can see I've got a lot to learn about the tropics.'

For an instant he seemed to unbend, and then he continued in the same imperious tone.

'Oh, and one other thing, Nurse . . .'

As Susan raised her eyes to his, she noticed that a thick strand of wavy fair hair had fallen over his forehead. He swept it back with a surprisingly boyish gesture of his hand as he said, 'It's not a good idea to pat the children on the head out here. Do remember that the refugees have travelled a long way and their sanitation is primitive, to say the least. One of the first things we do when admitting a patient into hospital is to treat the head.'

'Yes, Doctor,' Susan replied obediently, and breathed a sigh of relief as she heard his retreating footsteps on the harsh sand. Surely she must have heard wrongly? Nurse Hamlin had called him Dr Gregson. He couldn't possibly be *the* Dr Mike Gregson—the one Kate used to describe in her letters before she was married. She had seemed to be always talking about the handsome, fun-loving doctor with the infectious grin. At one point Susan had thought Kate would finish up marrying Mike Gregson—but no, it had always been Richard. Right from the moment she first met him . . .

Better concentrate, thought Susan as she

helped one tiny mite to hold his bowl steady. She looked around for his mother, but he appeared to be alone.

She called to one of the African nurses to take over the job of dispensing the food so that she could take the child across to the emergency annexe. Sister Obutu bustled forward, a pleasant smile on her dark, warm face.

'All alone, is he, Staff Nurse?' she asked kindly. 'I'll take care of him.' She spoke softly to the little boy in his own tongue as she took him by the hand.

Susan went back to her breakfast duty and carried on until all the refugees had been fed. By this time the sun's rays were intense, and she beat a hasty retreat into the comparative cool of the annexe.

The whirring of the electric fan in the middle of the ceiling mingled with the cries of the children and the occasional weary moaning of the mothers. Sister Obutu smiled as she came in.

'Ah, there you are, Nurse Bradshaw,' she beamed. 'Everything all right?'

'Yes, thank you, Sister.'

'Well, perhaps you'd like to come round with me this morning, and I'll try to show you the ropes.'

'I certainly would.' Susan felt relieved that Sister was going to take her under her wing. She certainly didn't want to be thrown in at the deep end on her first day. Three years training to State

Registration, followed by two years as a staff nurse on Paediatrics did not prevent her from feeling unsure of herself in the present situation.

'I thought I'd show you round the three main areas of the Emergency Annexe, which is where you'll be working,' Sister was saying briskly as she made her way through the outer office. 'This, of course, is the outpatient department. We encourage the refugees to wander in when they have a medical problem, so consequently we are open twenty-four hours, unlike the main part of the hospital, where the outpatient department has set hours for dealing with specific problems.'

'How long has the Emergency Annexe been in operation?' Susan asked, looking around her at the somewhat makeshift wooden structure.

'Only a few months,' said Sister. 'It just sort of evolved from our need to cope with the refugees arriving from the famine-stricken areas in the north. The drought has dried up their land and whole families drift south in search of food and help. When the men have settled their women and children in the refugee camp, they often return to their land, afraid that they will lose it. This is our mother and child unit.'

Sister led the way into a large room containing more women and children than beds and cots.

'These are the lucky ones—the children with mothers,' smiled Sister Obutu. She walked round the ward chatting to the mothers as she went, and it was obvious to Susan that she was loved and respected by all her patients.

They walked back through the outpatient section and into the children and babies unit.

'These are the motherless ones,' Sister Obutu explained, pausing by the first cot. 'You're going to be invaluable to us here, Nurse Bradshaw, because of your paediatric experience.'

'Well, I certainly hope so, Sister,' said Susan. 'That's why I volunteered to come out here.'

'That was very brave of you, Nurse, considering you have no experience of the tropics. Do you know anyone out here?'

'Yes, my friend Kate—she married Dr Richard Brooks a couple of years ago. You may remember . . .'

'Why of course,' Sister said delightedly. 'It was the wedding of the year! What a charming couple they are—and so much in love . . .' She sighed and then laughed merrily. 'Mustn't stand here chatting—I've got so much to do. Nurse Hamlin,' she called to the staff nurse who was bending over one of the cots. 'Would you like Nurse Bradshaw to help you with the dressings this morning?'

'Oh, yes please, Sister. I'm rushed off my feet,' was the muffled reply from behind the white mask. 'There's a sterile gown and mask in the steriliser room over there.' She waved an arm and pointed with her forceps towards a white-painted door half-way down the ward.

'Thanks,' said Susan, as she made towards the indicated room.

'I'll go back to my outpatients,' Sister said. 'But don't be afraid to come and ask my help, if you need it.'

She breezed out through the ward door and Susan started to scrub up before gowning. A young African nurse was carefully emptying one of the sterilisers. She paused, long-handled forceps still in her hand, to smile at Susan. The broad smile lit up her dark face and displayed perfect strong white teeth.

'Can I help you, Staff Nurse?' she asked with the soft Matalan accent which Susan was beginning to find very pleasant to listen to.

'Yes, you can, Nurse,' replied Susan thankfully. 'I need a sterile gown and mask.'

'Of course,' was the quiet, courteous reply. 'One moment, Staff Nurse. I've almost finished.'

Methodically the nurse removed the remaining instruments from the steriliser with the large forceps, placing them into sterile kidney dishes which she covered with a sterile towel. Her task finished, she carefully removed a gown from its packet and helped Susan, who was now scrubbed up, to put it on. With equal precision the dark hands put a mask over the lower part of Susan's face and deftly tied it behind her head.

The young nurse could sense that the new staff nurse was smiling by the twinkling look in her pretty blue eyes. She admired the elegant short blonde hairstyle—it looked as if it had been expensively cut. Someone had said this new staff nurse had trained in London. I wonder if I'll ever get myself to London, she thought as she opened the door for Susan to go back into the ward.

Nurse Hamlin looked up from the patient she was dressing. Susan saw that he was a young boy, about the same age as the burns case Dr Gregson had pointed out to her at the food station, but this one had extensive burns over both arms.

'What happened here?' she asked Nurse Hamlin.

'Who knows?' was the brief reply. 'With so many children running around the refugee camp, accidents are bound to happen near those lethal open fires.'

'I see you stick to the old, tried-and-tested techniques,' Susan said as she watched Nurse Hamlin place tulle gras over the wounds.

'What else can we do, under the circumstances?' came the curt reply.

'Oh, I wasn't meaning to criticise,' Susan put in hurriedly. 'I merely meant . . .'

'I know what you meant,' interrupted Nurse Hamlin, slightly mollified. 'You're finding the transition from an up-to-date London teaching hospital incredibly difficult.' She straightened up and looked Susan straight in the eyes.

'Why, yes, I suppose I am,' Susan faltered.

'Well, you'll just have to adapt,' said Nurse

Hamlin brusquely. 'I had to, when I first came out. Especially here in the Emergency Annexe—we are way behind the times. But we do the best we can for the patients.'

'I'm sorry, I . . .'

'No need to be sorry,' Nurse Hamlin said in a kindlier tone. 'Just remember to be adaptable. Now, would you like to finish the dressings for me?'

'Yes, of course.' Susan brightened visibly. At last she could use her professional expertise.

'Nurse Gusau makes a good runner,' said Nurse Hamlin, and the young nurse who was helping her smiled at the compliment.

'You can carry on with these burns cases here—five in all. Sulphonamide powder, tulle gras and bandages for all of them, please. If we could keep them in an aseptic air-conditioned treatment room, we should do so, but . . .' She raised her hands in a resigned gesture.

'Don't worry,' Susan smiled, as she prepared to take over. 'I'll adapt.'

'I'm sure you will . . .' Nurse Hamlin was already hurrying away. 'If you need me, I'm helping with the baby-feeds.'

The small boy watched Susan with big round eyes as she bandaged his arms.

'What's your name?' she asked gently as she put a piece of plaster across the end of the bandage.

The little boy did not reply, so Nurse Gusau

repeated the question in the Kulani dialect.

'Mbau,' he whispered shyly.

Susan smiled. 'Well, Mbau, your wound is beginning to heal nicely.'

A puzzled expression came over his dark face.

'Nurse Gusau, will you translate for me, please,' she asked.

What a blessing the African nurses are, she thought as she went across the ward to scrub for the next patient. As she pushed off the lever tap with her elbow, the swing doors opened and an all too familiar white-coated figure walked in. Susan was glad that the mask concealed her lower features, because she could feel the blood rushing to her face.

Dr Gregson turned towards her, noting the startled look in her expressive blue eyes.

'I was looking for Nurse Hamlin,' he said brusquely. 'Another small patient for you. He's very undernourished, as you can see. High protein diet . . .'

Susan glanced down at the young boy by Dr Gregson's side. It was the same child she had noticed alone in the food queue, and Sister had taken into Outpatients. She looked at her hands, still wet from scrubbing up.

'If you'll wait a minute, Doctor . . .'

'Haven't got a minute, Nurse,' he snapped. 'I realise you're supposed to be doing dressings, but you'll have to learn to do two things at once in

this place. This is Kyruba, *not* London. Ah,
Nurse Hamlin . . .'

Dr Gregson smiled at the capable figure
hurrying down the ward towards him.

'Perhaps you can help me.' He turned his back
on Susan, who returned to her dressings,
breathing deeply to overcome the profound
turmoil inside her. There must be some mistake—this arrogant man couldn't possibly be the
charming Dr Mike Gregson Kate had described
to her so often. On the other hand . . . She risked
a hasty glance across the ward and saw that Dr
Gregson was smiling at Nurse Hamlin. The smile
accentuated the laughter lines at the corner of his
deep blue eyes and wide, sensuous mouth. As
she bent over the next patient, she made a mental
note to ask Kate about him.

The morning passed very quickly for Susan.
There was so much to be done. No sooner had
she finished the dressings than it was time to help
with the two-hourly high-protein feeds to the
children suffering from malnutrition. She was so
absorbed in her task that she hadn't noticed the
time.

'Time to go to lunch, Susan,' Nurse Hamlin
reminded her.

'Good heavens, so it is! I'll just finish this feed,'
she said.

'No you won't.' Nurse Hamlin took the bowl.
'It's time you were off duty. You're on a two-five
today I believe?'

'Yes.'

'OK, I'll finish off here. You go away and enjoy yourself. Got anything to do this afternoon?'

'I've arranged to go out to Ogiwa to see Kate,' replied Susan as she stood up, smoothing down the starched white uniform and straightening her cap.

'That's nice. I'll see you at five then.' Nurse Hamlin had taken the small child on her lap and was coaxing open the thin lips. 'Nurse Gusau has a two-five, so she'll take you to lunch.'

Susan smiled gratefully at the young nurse who was waiting and followed her down the ward and out through the swing doors. The electric fans in the ward ceiling had managed to keep the temperature down somewhat; by contrast the long corridor leading through to the main hospital was unbearably hot. Nurse Gusau looked cool and unruffled, but Susan could feel that the cotton of her dress was sticky with perspiration.

'Phew, this heat is quite something,' she breathed as she walked along beside Nurse Gusau.

The dark face creased into a smile and Nurse Gusau said softly, 'You'll soon get used to it, Staff Nurse.'

'I certainly hope so,' said Susan. She was relieved to find that the dining-room was air-conditioned.

'We do make some concessions to the twentieth century,' Nurse Gusau said pleasantly, as they sat down at one of the round tables.

Each table was covered with a cloth and set for eight people. In the centre there was a small vase of fresh tropical flowers. It seemed strange to Susan that in the midst of all the pain and suffering of the emergency situation, conditions in the dining-room could be so normal. It helped to renew her sense of proportion and remind her that the outside world was waiting to be enjoyed.

A white-coated African steward served them with vegetable soup, pork chops, and a delicious fruit salad to finish with.

'Obviously the famine has not affected us here,' she said as she prepared to leave the table at the end of the meal.

'We are very lucky in Kyruba,' agreed Nurse Gusau. 'Being on the sea, we can always rely on imported foodstuffs during a drought, and there are emergency irrigation schemes near the town. These will be stretched to the limit, however, if the rains don't come soon. Do you think you are going to survive out here?'

Susan smiled at the young African nurse. 'I certainly intend to. It's something of a challenge, of course, but everyone has been so helpful . . . apart from . . .' She broke off in mid-sentence.

'Apart from . . . ?' prompted Nurse Gusau enquiringly.

Susan took a deep breath. 'Apart from that awful Dr Gregson . . .'

'Awful?' repeated Nurse Gusau. 'But he's gorgeous . . . Everyone adores him—patients and nurses alike.'

'Perhaps he just doesn't like me,' said Susan lamely.

'I agree he may be difficult to understand at first, but you'll soon find yourself falling for his charms.'

'Not me!' Susan said determinedly as she stood up from the table.

The two of them walked back to the nurses' home together. It was a white-painted two-storey building, set back from the hospital. Susan's room was on the first floor, from which there was an excellent view of the harbour. She paused for a few seconds to glance at the brightly-coloured boats bobbing on the blue water before hurrying along the corridor for a quick shower. Back in her room, she selected a cool yellow cotton dress and white strappy sandals. A hasty look at her watch told her that there was only just time to reach the hospital gates by two o'clock, so she picked up her shoulder bag and went quickly out of the door.

Richard's car was waiting for her by the hospital gates, as Kate had arranged. Susan knew immediately that the handsome, distinguished, dark-haired man must be Richard. Kate's description here had been faultless, but as for her description of Mike Gregson . . .

'Dr Brooks?' Susan drew level with the car.

The handsome features broke into a friendly smile. 'Please, call me Richard.' He leaned across and opened the door of the passenger seat. 'And you must be Susan.'

'Yes.' She climbed in beside Kate's husband and looked at him appraisingly. 'It's very good of you to give me a lift.'

'Not at all,' Richard said as he let in the clutch. 'I had to have lunch at the hospital today, and when Kate said you were coming out to visit her I seized the opportunity of going home for a couple of hours.'

'Well, just so long as I'm not causing you any inconvenience,' said Susan as the car sped along the marina.

'Inconvenience?' Richard laughed. 'You're doing me a favour. I had some boring paperwork to get through, but your visit has given me the excuse I need to spend the afternoon with my family.'

'How is Kate?' she asked.

'Fine . . . as lovely as ever,' Richard replied. 'Motherhood seems to suit her.'

'And young Jonathan?'

'Oh, he's amazing, of course . . .' He took his eyes from the wheel for an instant to look at her. 'I shall probably bore you to tears, going on about my son.'

They had stopped at traffic lights in the centre of Kyruba.

'Not at all,' Susan smiled. 'He sounds perfectly

wonderful, from Kate's letters.'

The lights changed and the car shot forward.

'I imagine Kate has a somewhat biased opinion too,' said Richard, as he skilfully negotiated the traffic. 'You'd better wait till you get out to Ogiwa House, and judge for yourself.'

'How old is he now?' Susan asked.

'Would you believe ten months?' said the proud father.

'Incredible . . . it seems only yesterday he was born.'

'It seems only yesterday that I first met Kate,' Richard added softly, a far-away look in his expressive grey eyes.

It must be wonderful to be so much in love, thought Susan wistfully. I thought I was in love once—not so long ago. But it couldn't have been love, could it? The feeling she'd had for Andrew when they first went out together had been exciting, but it soon faded. She hadn't wanted to spend her life with him, like Kate wanted Richard . . .

CHAPTER TWO

RICHARD AND SUSAN drove through the outskirts of Kyruba. The road became a long, bumpy track as they approached Ogiwa House, and then at last they drove through a wide gateway and round a gravel drive. The house was a two-storey building, made of stone. It looked out across a large garden to a magnificent view of the Ogiwa Dam. Susan thought it was quite breathtaking.

As she got out of the car and walked towards the house, Kate came rushing out and bounded down the steps.

'Susan!' she called as she ran across the gravel and threw her arms round her friend. 'Oh, it's so good to see you again! I can't believe you're actually here in Matala.'

'It's wonderful to be here,' said Susan, her blue eyes sparkling with happiness at the warm welcome. 'Let me look at you, Kate.' She held her at arm's length and then turned to Richard. 'You're quite right, Richard, motherhood does suit her—she looks radiant.'

'It's called love,' said Kate, with a laugh. 'I'm so lucky to have such a darling family and to live here in my favourite house . . .' She paused for breath, and Richard quickly said,

'Well, how about a kiss for your husband, then? I wondered when you'd notice me.'

'Darling, I'm sorry . . .' Kate reached up and kissed her husband fondly. 'It's so exciting having Susan here. Come inside, both of you. It's too hot to stand out here.'

After the sticky afternoon heat, the house seemed delightfully cool.

'Jonathan's having a rest at the moment, but he should be awake before you go,' said Kate as she led the way through the house. 'We'll sit on the veranda—it's nice and shady out here, and we can have a good gossip about the old days. I suppose things are changing back in London . . .'

Behind them Richard gave a discreet cough.

'I think I'll leave you ladies to your gossip,' he said, 'I've got some work to do in my study.'

'All right, my love.' Kate flashed him a happy smile. 'We don't want to bore you. Come and join us for some tea when you've finished.'

The two friends sat down on the veranda in comfortable basket chairs.

'What a marvellous view, Kate,' Susan commented.

'Yes, isn't it.' Kate sighed happily as she looked out across the garden to the distant palm trees which surrounded the Ogiwa Dam.

It was utterly peaceful; no sound broke the stillness of the afternoon. Everything seemed to be asleep. There was not a breath of wind—not a ripple on the water . . .

'You must be very happy,' Susan said.

'Yes, I am,' Kate replied simply. 'Sometimes I pinch myself to make sure it's not a dream.'

'I must say you look extremely well. I like the new hairstyle.'

'Oh that . . .' Kate ran a hand through the short, dark, well-cut hair. 'I just had to have my long hair cut when I was expecting Jonathan. It was so hot, and I was always having to pin it up on top of my head. This is much easier. Now, tell me about yourself. How are you settling in at Kyruba?'

'Oh, quite well . . . quite well,' Susan said carefully.

'You don't sound too sure. Is anything the matter?' said Kate quickly.

'No—well, not really . . . It's just that I really can't seem to get on with Dr Gregson.' The last part of Susan's words came out in a rush.

'Mike?' asked Kate incredulously. 'You don't mean Mike?'

'I think I do,' Susan nodded slowly. 'He's in charge of the Emergency Annexe . . .'

'Tall, good-looking, fair hair, blue eyes, always got a grin on his face . . .' Kate burst in.

'Well, I don't know about the grin, but I suppose the rest is true,' Susan admitted reflectively.

'Oh, but he's adorable,' said Kate. 'He was

marvellous to me when I first came out here. I must have told you about him in my letters.'

'Yes you did . . . I just didn't recognise the description, that's all.' Susan was quiet.

'Oh, you'll soon get used to Mike,' said Kate. 'Although, I must admit, I heard he'd changed somewhat since I first knew him. He's much more serious, apparently; works too hard, Richard says. Come to think of it, I haven't seen him for ages. He never comes out here, and I rarely go down to the hospital.'

'Perhaps I'll get used to his abrupt manner,' said Susan hopefully.

'You really do surprise me.' Kate looked confused. 'I can't believe we're talking about the same man. We used to have such fun together. He was always dreaming up some exciting place to take me in my off-duty . . . He went back to the UK soon after Richard and I were married, to do a paediatrics course. After he came back he was put in charge of the Emergency Annexe, and he seems to spend a lot of time there. Apart from going out with his girlfriend.'

'Oh, he has a girlfriend then?' Susan asked, beginning to feel interested, in spite of herself.

'So Richard tells me,' said Kate. 'I've never met her myself, but I've heard her voice.'

Susan looked puzzled.

'I'm sorry,' laughed Kate. 'I should have explained. She's a radio announcer with the Matala Broadcasting Corporation—quite a celebrity, I believe. We haven't got television in Matala yet, so the radio is important if you want to keep in touch with the rest of the world.'

'Yes, I suppose it is,' Susan sounded thoughtful. A child's cry sounded from upstairs, and Kate's face lit up.

'That's Jonathan. I'll bring him down.'

Susan watched as her friend hurried inside the house. Kate certainly didn't seem any older than when they had started their training together, five years ago, in London. Moments later she emerged from the house carrying her precious bundle. Jonathan was rubbing his eyes sleepily, and at first he seemed surprised to see a stranger. Then his little face creased into a big smile and he held out his hands.

Susan laughed as she reached forward to take him in her arms.

'What a friendly little boy you are,' she said happily as he snuggled against her.

'My, we are honoured,' his proud mother laughed. 'He doesn't take to everyone so quickly. He can see that you like children.'

'Years of practice,' smiled Susan. 'I think I'll probably specialise in paediatrics when I go back to London.'

'How about having some of your own?' queried Kate, mischievously.

'Aren't you rather putting the cart before the horse? I've got to find a husband first.'

'I wouldn't have thought that would present

any problems,' Kate said, with a wry laugh. 'What's happened to the delectable Andrew you told me about?'

'Oh, that was just a flash in the pan,' Susan said hurriedly. 'We were just good friends. Andrew was fun to be with, but I never contemplated spending my whole life with him.'

'I know what you mean,' said Kate helpfully. 'Funnily enough I used to feel like that about Mike Gregson—we were just good friends. But with Richard . . .'

She paused, and the two friends laughed.

'Honestly, Susan, I sometimes feel so much in love that I can hardly breathe,' Kate said softly. 'Oh, you'll recognise the signs and symptoms of true love when you meet the right man . . . no mistaking it. But why the past tense where Dr Andrew is concerned?'

'Because he's gone to work in the States—so that's that,' Susan said firmly and, she hoped, convincingly.

'Mm . . .' Kate looked doubtful as she watched her friend. 'Maybe it is . . . We shall see.'

'Honestly, Kate—it's finished. Ouch! Jonathan, that's my hair you're pulling!'

Kate laughed. 'He's fascinated by the colour—I don't think he's seen real blonde hair before, apart from his own. Here . . . let me take him. I'll put him in his play-pen. He gets very hot if we hold him for too long. There you are, Jonathan.'

She put her son down in the large play-pen near their chairs. He gurgled happily as he started to play with some brightly-coloured bricks. First he piled them on top of each other, then knocked them down with a wild sweep of his chubby little hands. He played happily throughout the afternoon while they chatted.

Kate was watching him fondly when she said, 'Funny, you know, I can't imagine life now without Jonathan and Richard . . . Talking of Richard, shall we see if we can disturb him? Muhammadu!' she called to a steward in a white tunic with a small round green pill-box hat, denoting he belonged to the Hausa tribe.

'Madam?' He came out on to the veranda.

'Could we have some tea, please, and would you ask the doctor if he would like to join us?'

'Yes, madam.' The steward moved silently away, into the house, and very soon afterwards Richard appeared.

'Ah, there you are, darling,' said Kate. 'Have you finished your work?'

'No, but I don't mind being disturbed by two beautiful girls.' With a smile, he dropped a light kiss on his wife's cheek.

'Flattery will get you everywhere,' said Kate with a knowing grin. 'We were discussing Mike . . .'

Susan looked startled. 'Well, he just came into the conversation . . .'

'Yes, but you seemed worried to me,' Kate

said. 'How do you find him these days, Richard?'

'He seems fine—under a lot of pressure at the hospital, but now you come to mention it, I think he does take on more work than he should . . . He's certainly much more serious than he used to be.' Richard looked quizzically across at Susan, who coloured embarrassingly under the searching grey eyes.

'Have you had problems with him?' he asked directly.

'No, not really . . .' Susan paused uncomfortably. 'He's rather abrupt, that's all . . . Can I lift Jonathan out of his play-pen?' She stood up and lifted the little boy into her arms, wishing she'd never mentioned the name Mike Gregson.

Muhammadu came out with the tea tray, and Susan was able to cover up her confusion in the ensuing activity. Carefully she poured orange juice into Jonathan's cup and helped him to swallow it down thirstily. He held out the empty cup for more when it was finished, and she was kept busy as she tried to amuse him at the table.

'You've hardly touched your tea,' said Kate. 'Here, let me take Jonathan.' The little boy sat happily on his mother's lap, banging a teaspoon on the table.

'What a noisy boy you are, Jonathan,' said his father dotingly. 'And to think I came home for a bit of peace and quiet . . . We'll have to go soon, Susan, if I'm to get you back on duty by five o'clock.'

She sighed. 'No peace for the wicked! It's been a lovely afternoon, Kate.'

'Well, you must come again soon—whenever you can make it,' Kate said. 'You're always welcome.'

They all strolled back to the car, Kate carrying Jonathan on her hip in true African style. Susan bent down to give the little boy a kiss on the cheek.

'He's such a picture,' she laughed. 'It's so unusual to have blonde hair and a sun-tan like he's got.'

'Yes, he loves the sun, but I have to be very careful in the middle of the day, otherwise he'd burn. His hair is bleached by the sun, of course. I think it'll darken as he grows older.'

Richard opened the door and Susan climbed in. They said their goodbyes and the car sped off down the drive. Susan turned for a last glimpse of Kate and Jonathan standing in front of the house.

'And they lived happily ever after . . .' she murmured, almost to herself.

Richard smiled and glanced across. 'Yes, I think you could say that,' he said quietly.

They drove along the unmade track towards the main Kyruba road. Susan was lost in thought and found herself jerked back to reality when Richard added, 'So, you're not too keen on our friend Mike Gregson?'

'I've only just met him—I expect it takes time to get to know him . . .'

'Oh, I'm sure you're right about that,' said Richard. 'And he does rather immerse himself in his work nowadays. That, and his girlfriend, Janice.'

'Oh yes, his girlfriend. Kate was telling me about her.'

'Quite a startling character—very glamorous. I expect you'll meet her at the charity do,' Richard said as he swung the car on to the main road and changed up into top gear.

'Charity do?' enquired Susan.

'Oh, sorry, my dear; I was forgetting you've only just arrived,' he said. 'Janice is arranging a big charity concert this week—lots of her show-biz friends are flying out here in aid of the Famine Relief Fund.'

'Oh, I see . . . how nice,' Susan responded lamely. She glanced at her watch. 'Heavens! We'll only just make it.'

'Don't worry,' Richard laughed as he guided the car expertly past a slow-moving mammy-wagon, which was crowded with refugees from the drought-stricken northern territories. 'I'll get you back on time.'

They reached the town and the car wove in and out of the tortuous traffic in the narrow crowded streets. By the time they reached the hospital there were only minutes to spare. Susan thanked Richard before rushing to her room to change into her uniform. It was literally on the stroke of five as she pushed open the swing doors of the paediatric unit.

A pair of hostile blue eyes fixed themselves upon her as Mike Gregson walked down between the rows of cots and beds. As he drew level with her he paused and said quietly, 'In the nick of time, I see, Nurse. Not a minute to spare.'

Susan wasn't sure whether he was paying her a compliment or merely being sarcastic. She glanced at the big clock on the wall, and was relieved to see that she wasn't late.

'Well, it's good of you to join us, I must say,' he continued in the same inscrutable tone of voice. 'Did you have a pleasant afternoon?'

Surprised at his interest, Susan raised her eyes to his, but saw nothing other than a blank, neutral expression.

'Yes thank you, Doctor. I went to see my friend Kate.' It was out before she could stop herself. She hadn't meant to be so forthcoming.

'Ah, Kate,' he repeated absently. 'You are referring to Dr Brook's wife, I presume.'

'Yes, we trained together,' she answered politely.

'Did you indeed?' The stern eyes swept over her, almost caressingly, before Dr Gregson turned abruptly. 'Sister will need your help with the babies, I think.'

He pushed open the swing doors and was gone.

Susan took a deep breath and headed off down

the ward towards the babies' section at the end. She paused for a quick word with Mbau, who was sitting up in bed pushing a toy car backwards and forwards across the sheet with his feet, having been forbidden to use his bandaged arms. He smiled cheerily at her. She noticed that the little boy she had admitted that morning had been put in the bed next to him. He was extremely thin and gave no flicker of recognition when she stopped to speak to him. Acute malnutrition, she thought. He's going to need all the help we can give, if he's to survive. High protein diet—but I'd better find Sister first . . .

Sister was sitting in the middle of the babies' section feeding one of the tiny infants, a pleasant, if somewhat harassed, smile on her face.

'Oh, thank goodness you're back, Nurse. Feeds, please—they're already made up in the feeds kitchen. There's a chart in there—go and have a look.'

Susan went into the small, spotlessly clean room which served as a kitchen for making up the feeds. It was well-organised. Each baby had its own chart listing the recommended feed in one column and the actual amount consumed in the next. There was a cupboard containing all the ingredients for the feeds, a refrigerator, bottle steriliser and also a shelf for EBM milk—expressed breast milk. Susan was pleased to see that there was a breast milk bank, although she thought that some of it would be of doubtful nutritional value, having seen the malnourished state of some of the mothers.

She picked up a chart and the appropriate bottle before going back into the ward. Putting the bottle down on the table at the side of a cot, she lifted the white gown from its hook and put it over her uniform. Each baby had its own gown for the nurses to wear, to prevent cross-infection.

Two tiny brown eyes gazed appealingly up at her as she reached down into the cot to pick up the dusky-skinned baby. The weak, grizzling sound he had been making stopped, and the baby waited with unusual calm to see what would happen next. So different to the well-nourished babies in the UK, thought Susan. These dear little scraps are much too quiet and resigned.

Gently she removed the moist napkin before swabbing the tiny brown buttocks. After applying some zinc oxide powder, she put on a clean Harrington square. When she had washed her hands again, she cuddled the baby into the crook of her left arm and inserted the bottle teat carefully into his mouth. At first he wasn't interested in the nourishing liquid, but Susan talked softly to him, looking gently all the time into the tiny beseeching eyes.

Suddenly the little mite started to suck and she breathed a sigh of relief. As she did so she was aware that Sister had come up behind her and was watching her.

'Well done, Nurse,' Sister said quietly. 'He's

not an easy feeder—you did right to persist with him. It's the only way. I can see you like babies, don't you.'

It was a statement, not a question, but Susan nodded as she concentrated all her attention on this delicate scrap of humanity who depended on her for survival. This is what real nursing is all about, she thought.

'I'll leave you in charge of the babies for the moment,' said Sister. 'You've got two nurses to help you. I shall be in the mother and baby unit if you need me . . .'

She bustled off down the ward, beaming all over her face. It was obvious she was pleased with her new staff nurse.

Susan and the other nurses worked methodically throughout the evening, feeding and changing the babies and checking the saline drips of those who couldn't feed naturally. She went to the dining-room for supper at half-past seven and was back again at eight for the final clearing-up session before the night staff arrived. Most of the babies were settled, so she helped Sister in the mother and baby section.

As many mothers as possible were given beds near to their children, but some had to sleep on mats on the floor.

'It's no hardship for them, Nurse Bradshaw,' Sister said kindly when she saw Susan looking surprised at the simplicity of the accommodation. 'Many have travelled for days through the bush to reach us. This probably seems like luxury.'

The ward was becoming quieter now as the mothers and children settled down for the night. A peaceful hush rested over the large room. Outside, night had fallen, and Susan could hear the sounds of the insects droning in the hospital garden.

'No need for any sedatives here, Sister,' she whispered with a smile. 'Makes quite a change from UK nursing.'

'Yes, I'm sure it does.'

'I'll go back and see how the babies are.' Susan turned to leave. As she did so, the door by Sister's desk opened and a dark-haired young man in a white coat walked in.

'Ah, Dr Collins, I wanted to see you,' Sister said, rising from her desk. 'I don't believe you've met Nurse Bradshaw, have you?'

The deep brown eyes in the handsome face swept over Susan with an appraising glance.

'No, you're quite right, Sister. We haven't met, otherwise I would have remembered,' Dr Collins said smoothly.

'Nurse Bradshaw has just joined us,' continued Sister. 'A valuable new member of the team, I think.'

'That's good news,' the young doctor nodded, his eyes still on Susan.

'Yes, isn't it,' Sister said absently. 'Now, Dr Collins, I wanted your advice . . .'

Susan went quickly out of the door and back to the babies' unit, where Nurse Gusau was doing the final feed. She sat down at the desk to check the feed charts and write up the report.

What a pleasant young man Dr Collins seems, she thought as she put down her pen. At least that was one doctor she wouldn't mind seeing again. As the ward doors opened she turned, half hoping for another meeting with Dr Collins, but her pulse quickened. He stood in the doorway, but he was not alone. The tall, imperious figure at his side bore down on her.

'I wasn't aware that you were in charge here, Nurse,' he said ominously.

Susan stood up quickly.

'I'm holding the fort for Sister,' she said defensively.

'On your first evening?' Dr Gregson queried. 'My my, Sister must have great faith in you.'

'She seems to be very pleased with Nurse Bradshaw, from what I can gather,' put in Dr Collins quietly.

Dr Gregson turned to look at his colleague in surprise. 'I didn't know you two had met,' he said.

'Only briefly,' Dr Collins added. 'But I did ask Sister to tell me something about Nurse Bradshaw,' he admitted with a wry grin.

'Did you indeed.' A suspicion of a smile played on Dr Gregson's full, sensuous lips, lightening the stern expression on his handsome face.

Susan waited for the smile to develop, but his face clouded over again and he said quickly, 'Well, Dave, perhaps you'd like to check the feed charts for me. I'm sure it would be no hardship for you under the circumstances.' He paused for a moment and his deep blue eyes met Susan's. She turned away hurriedly, and he continued, 'I do have an appointment, so I'll leave you to it.'

'Of course,' said Dave Collins happily. Without another word, Mike Gregson turned and left the ward.

'Well, where would you like to begin, Doctor?' Susan asked in her super-professional voice.

'Let's get the work done first,' he smiled. 'And then perhaps we could wander off for a quiet drink somewhere.'

'Not tonight,' Susan said hurriedly. 'I'm absolutely whacked. Let's just check the charts, see to the babies and . . . ah, Sister.'

Sister came floating in, still looking full of energy. 'That's all right, Nurse. It's time you were off duty. I'll take care of Dr Collins.'

He gave Susan a wry grin as he settled himself at the desk beside Sister.

Susan walked out through the main door of the Emergency Annexe and crossed the compound to the nurses' home. High in the sky, a bright new moon was shining down, lighting up the yellow sand of the compound. The soft fragrance of tropical roses and frangipani was wafting over from the hospital garden, and all around her she could hear the soft click of the insects scurrying beneath the palm trees.

West Africa . . . Matala . . . it was everything she had ever thought it would be . . . and more, oh, much more!

The cool white sheets of her narrow bed beckoned her invitingly as she closed the door in her room. Stripping off her white uniform she crawled between them and was very soon asleep.

In her dreams there was a tall handsome man with deep blue eyes and unruly fair hair, which kept dropping down over his forehead. When he smiled at her his whole face lit up in infectious laughter. He was happy and carefree, and she felt she had known him a long time. But who was he?

She awoke in the soft darkness of the tropical night. What a strange dream . . . Whoever was that she had been dreaming about? Pulling the sheet over her head, she tried to sleep again . . .

CHAPTER THREE

WHEN SUSAN awoke, the hot tropical sun was streaming in through the window of her room, even though it was still early. She looked about her trying to remember where she was. The memory of that dream lingered with her . . . The fair haired man—who could he be? It wasn't— no, surely not! Mike Gregson never smiled at her with that radiant, adoring look . . . Quite the reverse. Was it Andrew? No, she didn't think so . . .

She shivered, in spite of the early morning heat, and climbed out of bed. Crossing to the window she opened it wide and stared out at the activity down on the harbour. Boats of all description were tied up, and the people on board were beginning their day. Some of the fishing boats were already making their way out to the open sea. A huge luxury liner, anchored near the mouth of the harbour, was preparing to discharge a party of gaudily-clad tourists who, no doubt, wanted to know what a primitive country really looked like. They would be able to go home and say they had 'done' Matala.

Susan smiled to herself as she wondered how long it would take to get used to living here. She put on her bathrobe and went along the corridor for a quick shower. The cascading water was refreshing, and removed any lingering memories of her dream. Back in her room, she tossed yesterday's crumpled uniform into the linen basket and selected another impeccably starched and ironed dress. Thank goodness they have a good laundry here, she thought, as she smoothed down her uniform in front of the mirror. She pinned the little white cap on top of her blonde head and went quickly off to breakfast in the hospital dining-room.

This was a relatively simple meal—not the usual cooked affair served up in UK hospitals. Presumably we don't need so many calories to keep us warm, she thought incongruously, as she finished her fresh grapefruit and a slice of toast.

Sister Obutu was already working at her desk when Susan arrived at the Emergency Annexe.

'Good morning, Nurse Bradshaw,' she said with a cheery smile. 'Come and sit down—I'll give you a report before you start work. Pull up a chair.'

Susan sat down and made notes on the cases relevant to her own work. The most alarming aspect was the admission of two children with measles.

'Measles?' she exclaimed in alarm. 'But I thought that was extremely rare out here?'

'It is,' said Sister. 'But when it strikes it can reach epidemic proportions. It's especially dangerous when combined with malnutrition, as we have here. Strict barrier nursing is essential, of course—I've put the two girls in a side ward. Fortunately the mother brought them straight here when she arrived after a long, exhausting journey from the north. They haven't been in the refugee camp at all, so if we can contain the disease here, we shall escape an epidemic.'

Her expressive brown eyes looked at Susan.

'I'll do my best, Sister.' Susan stood up to start work. 'Oh, by the way, any news of the mother of that little boy I admitted yesterday—the one who was all alone in the food queue?'

Sister smiled happily. 'Yes—we tracked her down in Maternity. She had a little girl last night. I'm having her transferred to us this morning, so her son will be able to join us soon.'

'That's good news. Does he know?'

'Yes, I told him earlier on,' Sister said. 'He's brightened up considerably since then—still rather weak though; keep pushing fluids.'

'Yes, of course, Sister.' Susan made her way through to the children's ward. The unmistakable early-morning cries from the babies always reminded her of lambs in a field back home in England. She smiled to herself at the thought, but the vision soon vanished as she started work.

Nurse Gusau and another nurse were feeding the babies. Susan went into the side ward and put on a gown and mask. The two little girls with measles were sitting up in bed looking miserable.

There was no mistaking the dusky red, maculo-papular eruption which covered their bodies, and the bloated bleary-eyed appearance of their faces. A couple of breakfast bowls of *gari*, on the side tables, lay untouched.

Susan sat down between the two girls and started to coax some food into them. Little by little some of the food disappeared, but it was an uphill battle. She spent a few more minutes persuading them to drink before deciding to leave them to rest for a while.

At least the most infectious period is over, now that the rash is fully out, Susan thought as she scrubbed her hands. They will be infectious for about another week, so if only we can contain the illness all will be well.

She went down the ward towards the ster-iliser room. As she passed the young boy whose mother was in Maternity she smiled, and to her surprise the emaciated brown features smiled back. She paused and went across to his bedside.

'I've just heard the good news,' she said, smil-ing happily. 'A baby sister, isn't it?' As she said this, Susan made rocking movements with her arms to indicate, she hoped, what looked like a baby.

Obviously the young boy understood because his smile broadened and he said something to Susan in the soft, undulating tones of the Kulani tribe.

I wish I knew what he was saying, thought Susan and, as if by magic, a deep masculine voice behind her said, 'Uwaya wants to thank you for your help, Nurse.'

Susan turned in surprise, and as she did so her hand brushed the hand of the man standing behind her. An electrifying feeling passed through her body as she found herself confronted by the tall fair-haired figure. Those blue eyes staring at her—where had she seen them before? They were so blue she felt as if she were drowning in them.

Dr Gregson broke the spell, saying gently, 'Our little patient is very grateful, Nurse Bradshaw.'

'Oh, but I really haven't done anything, Doctor. I simply noticed he was on his own and, well . . .' She stopped, feeling embarrassed at his change in attitude.

He was actually smiling at her, not only with his lips, but also with his eyes. Her legs felt as if they were turning to jelly. What was it Kate had said about the signs and symptoms of love . . .? No, she was confusing this man with the image in her dream. They were entirely different. The facial features were similar but . . .

Already Mike Gregson's smile had vanished.

'I need some help setting up a drip over there, Nurse,' he was saying in a cool, professional voice. 'Could you bring me a sterile trolley, as quickly as possible.'

'Of course, Doctor.'

Susan headed for the steriliser room and returned to the bedside by the time Mike had finished scrubbing up. He was coaxing the tiny blue vein in the emaciated brown arm of a little Kulani girl, a frown of deep concentration on his face.

'Almost ready, my dear . . . There we are, that's fine. Just a little prick,' he said as he took the cannula from Susan and inserted it expertly into the exposed vein.

As Susan hung the bottle of glucose saline on the stand and regulated the flow, she was aware that two deep blue eyes were watching her, but her steady hands gave no indication of the effect they had upon her.

'Thank you, Nurse,' he said quietly as she finished.

Susan didn't dare to meet his gaze. She nodded almost imperceptibly and busied herself with settling her young patient. When she looked up he had gone.

For the rest of the day she was busy with dressings, feeds and medicines. She asked Nurse Gusau to special the measles cases and made sure that she knew what was involved. By the end of the afternoon she found herself looking forward to her evening off duty. What should she do with it? Was it too late to ring Kate?

She looked up from the baby she was feeding as the swing doors opened to reveal the welcome figure of Dave Collins. When he saw Susan, his face creased into a broad grin.

'I hoped I'd find you here. What time are you off duty?' he asked without further preamble.

'About five,' Susan said, while gently rubbing the baby's back to make him burp. 'Good boy,' she smiled as the required sound emerged.

'Who, me?' asked Dave, with mock hopefulness.

They both laughed, and he ran a nervous hand through his short dark hair before announcing, 'I'd like to take you out then—make it quarter to five and it's a date.'

'You're very sure of yourself, Doctor,' said Susan. 'Hand me that nappy-pin, please. Obediently Dave complied, while his brown eyes searched hers for an answer.

'Why quarter to five?' she asked, drawing out the time before she need say yes or no.

'Because that would give us time to get out to Ikawa for a swim in the pool before sunset,' he said quickly.

'Ikawa?' queried Susan.

'Yes, it's a nursing home, about half an hour's drive from here . . .'

'Oh yes, I know where you mean,' Susan said as she wrapped the nappy round her little patient. 'Kate used to work there.'

'Yes, that's right . . . Well, are you coming?'

He watched as, with studied deliberation, Susan placed the tiny baby gently back in his cot and tucked the cotton sheet round him. 'I might,' she said with a smile, as she straightened up. 'But I'll have to stay till fivc.'

'Nonsense! I've already asked Sister . . . Oops!' He paused in embarrassment.

'You were pretty confident I'd come with you, then,' Susan said, her blue eyes twinkling. 'What would you have done if I'd said no?'

He grinned mischievously. 'I should have looked around for another beautiful blonde— there must be lots of them in Kyruba.'

'OK, you win,' she agreed removing her white gown and hanging it beside the cot. 'But you're sure Sister said quarter to five was all right?'

'Of course I'm sure. She's sending Nurse Hamlin to take over from you.'

As if on cue, the tall auburn-haired staff nurse came through the swing doors.

'Talk of the devil,' said Dave with a grin.

'I thought my ears were burning,' she laughed. 'What were you two saying about me just then?'

'Nothing at all, my dear,' smiled Dave. 'Except how welcome you are at this particular moment in time. I'm about to initiate Nurse Bradshaw into the mysteries of the Ikawa pool.'

'Oh, lucky you,' said Monica Hamlin. 'Do I get a report first, Susan?'

'Of course—be with you in a few minutes, Dave,' Susan said, as she and Monica walked over to the desk.

'Meet me out front, as soon as you can,' he called as he went out.

The two staff nurses sat down at the desk and pored over the charts. It was a full ten minutes before Susan could get away to her room to change. Quickly she pulled off her uniform, stuffed it into the laundry bin and reached for the first thing that came to hand—cool white slacks and a sleeveless pale blue cotton top. As she ran a comb quickly through her hair, Susan felt pleased that she'd had it cut short. She grabbed her bikini and a towel and made for the door.

Dave was waiting impatiently by the main gate in a dark blue saloon. In spite of the fact that all the windows were down, he appeared red-faced and uncomfortable.

'Come on, Susan. I'm cooking inside this oven of a car,' he called.

'Sorry, Dave. I couldn't get away before now.'

'That's OK. Jump in.' He leaned over and opened the passenger door.

It was unbearably hot inside the small car, but as they gathered speed the air rushed through the side windows and helped to bring the temperature down. The road became rough and bumpy as they left the town and climbed towards Ikawa. Susan caught a glimpse of Ogiwa House set back amid the palm trees, before the road curved out of sight. Dave slowed the car to a steady pace as they reached the nursing home. Soon they were turning through the gateway and motoring up a short drive, with tall palm trees on either side. The car stopped in front of a long, low, colonial-style building. A veranda ran along the front of the house, from which wide wooden steps led down to the drive.

Susan got out and stood at the bottom of the steps, looking out across the garden. It was a very beautiful situation for a nursing home. She remembered Kate telling her about it. Dave joined her by the steps, just as a steward came out of the house.

'Ah, Musa,' said Dave with a friendly smile. 'Is Dr Miller anywhere around?'

'No, sir. He went to Kyruba, sir, but Nurse Smith is here.'

'Oh, well perhaps you could find Nurse Smith, Musa?'

'Nurse Smith is in the swimming pool, sir.'

'Splendid. That's what I'd hoped,' said Dave. 'We'll join her round the back—thank you, Musa. We can find our way there.'

'Yes, sir,' said Musa as he withdrew into the house.

'Siesta-time lasts until the evening out here,' said Dave with a grin. 'Come, on, Susan, follow me.'

He led the way round to the back of the nursing home. The sound of laughter and splashing told them they must be near the pool. Through the trees Susan caught a glimpse of dazzling blue water and then, as they emerged through the clearing, she saw two people sitting on the edge of the swimming pool, heads thrown back towards the dying rays of the late-afternoon sun.

'Julie!' called Dave.

The small, fair-haired young woman looked up when she heard her name. 'Dave,' she cried. 'Come along over. It's lovely and cool in the water.'

Susan gave a start as they neared the pool. Julie's companion had opened his deep blue eyes and was languidly surveying the approaching pair. To Susan's amazement she recognized Mike Gregson. She had never seen him outside the hospital—never seen him without the familiar white coat. The sleek black swimming trunks fitted perfectly over his athletic body, and the sight of his strong, rippling muscles had a peculiar effect on her. It was almost as if she could feel those skilful brown arms reaching out towards her . . .

She took a deep breath and waited to take her cue from Dave. Perfectly at ease with the situation, he introduced Susan to Julie, and Susan quickly explained that she was a friend of Kate's.

'I think I could safely say the old cliché—I've heard so much about you, Julie,' said Susan, now fully in control of herself again.

Julie smiled. 'Yes, Kate told me you were coming out. How are you settling in at Kyruba?'

'Oh, it's not too bad,' she said quietly, aware of those deep blue eyes on her face.

'What she means is, it's a million light-years from nursing in London,' Mike Gregson corrected with a sardonic smile.

'It certainly is different,' agreed Susan quickly, and her blue eyes looked straight at him. 'But then I knew it would be, and I didn't think it would be easy. It's just a question of adapting . . .'

'And I should say you're adapting very well, Susan,' put in Dave as he saw the look of annoyance creeping over her face. 'Anyway, we're not here to talk shop, and we're wasting valuable daylight.'

'Yes, why don't you two get changed and then we'll all have a swim,' suggested Julie.

Mike pulled himself to his full height. 'I've got to go now,' he said. 'Duty calls.'

'Oh, must you go so soon Mike? I thought we could have a drink . . .'

'I'm afraid not.' He strolled across and went into one of the changing-rooms. Susan watched as the tall, athletic figure disappeared.

'Which one shall I use, Julie?' she asked.

'Any one—apart from Mike's,' Julie added with a laugh.

Susan went into the nearest changing-room and slipped out of her clothes into her bikini. It was made of white cotton, and there wasn't much of it. She waited until she thought she heard a car start before daring to emerge.

Dave and Julie were already splashing around

in the pool. 'Come on, slowcoach,' called Dave. 'It'll soon be dark.'

Sure enough, Susan noticed that the red sun was low on the horizon. The twilight would soon be upon them, followed very quickly by the dark tropical night. She padded along to the deep end and dived in. The cool water refreshed her and took away the tiredness of the day as she swam steadily towards the shallow end and then back again. A few lengths of the pool and I shall have completely forgotten that arrogant, supercilious Dr Gregson, she thought. I wish I didn't have to keep meeting him. It's so unnerving . . .

She had swum several lengths before she was aware of Julie calling to her from the edge of the pool. 'Susan . . . Susan!'

She raised her head and looked across at the small fair-haired figure crouching by the pool.

'Susan—wherever were you? I've been trying to attract your attention.'

'Sorry, Julie—I was miles away,' she called as she turned to swim over.

'When you've had enough, come and join us for a drink,' Julie said.

'Thanks, I will.' Another couple of lengths would wash that man out of her thoughts . . .

When she joined the other two they looked up at her enquiringly. 'You seemed to enjoy that,' Julie said. 'You're a keen swimmer, I see.'

'I find it very relaxing.' Susan lowered herself on to a chair as Musa came towards the table.

'What will you have?' Julie asked.

'Something cool,' said Susan. 'Do you have any orange juice?'

'Of course madam.' Musa glided away with the minimum of fuss.

'You realise he's going to squeeze you some fresh juice and add ice cubes and all the trimmings,' said Julie.

'Really?' Susan's eyes were wide. 'You seem to have a very good life out here.'

'Can't grumble,' she said with a smile. 'Dr Miller is very good to work for.'

'Yes, where is he?' asked Dave.

'He's taken his wife and children into Kyruba to do some shopping. They won't be late,' Julie explained.

'Well, I'm afraid I won't be able to see him this time. We're pretty busy at the hospital,' Dave said with a wry grin. 'Not like this holiday camp.'

'Not so much of the holiday camp, if you please. I'm sure you could stay longer if you really wanted to. Musa cooks a very good supper, don't you, Musa?' Julie appealed to the steward who had just placed Susan's delicious-looking drink in front of her.

He smiled a broad, easy smile, revealing his even, pearly-white teeth. The linguistic complications of the reply were too difficult for him, so he merely nodded and said softly, 'Yes, madam,' before hurrying away.

'My big white chief will be waiting for me to get

back, Julie,' Dave said in a resigned voice.

'Oh, you mean dear old Mike,' she laughed easily.

'Dear old Mike,' repeated Dave, raising an eyebrow at Julie's tone of familiarity. 'I don't think he'd approve of you calling him that.'

'Why ever not?' she demanded. 'You forget, I've known him longer than you.'

'That still doesn't mean you can refer to him as "dear old Mike",' said Dave.

Julie gave a short sharp laugh. 'When I first knew Mike he was carefree, happy-go-lucky, fun-loving—and then . . .' She paused and looked at Susan.

'And then what?' asked Susan.

'And then . . . something happened.'

'Something happened?' queried Dave. 'What do you mean, *something happened*?'

'Well, I think his heart was broken,' Julie said quietly.

Dave laughed loudly and derisively. 'Now I've heard everything,' he said with a mocking sneer. 'A grown woman talking about somebody having their heart broken . . .'

'It's not funny, Dave,' interrupted Julie, so vehemently that he became quiet again.

'Look,' he continued after a few seconds, 'I think you're an incurable romantic, but you're also a qualified nurse. You should know that the anatomy and physiology of the heart do not allow for it to be broken. The heart can be . . .'

'Stop it, Dave,' said Susan firmly. 'There are some things that can't be explained scientifically. Julie's obviously given this a great deal of thought.'

Julie looked at her gratefully. 'Yes, you're right, Susan,' she said. 'I gave it a lot of thought a couple of years ago when Kate got married.'

'Kate? What has she got to do with it?'

'Look, Susan . . . I know Kate is your friend, but you must never tell her this, because she has absolutely no idea just how much Mike loved her. When she married Richard I think it broke his heart . . .'

This time Dave didn't laugh. He kept his gaze steadily out over the water, and it was Susan who broke the silence.

'But why do you think this, Julie?' she asked softly.

'Because he's so different now. He refuses to become emotionally involved. He's still a first-class doctor, but as for his personal life—well, I mean you've only got to look at that girlfriend of his . . .'

'What's wrong with her?' Susan asked innocently.

'Oh, there's nothing wrong with her,' Julie responded. 'It's just that . . . well, Dave, you know her, don't you?'

Dave nodded, intrigued at Julie's revelations.

'Don't you think she looks a bit like Kate?'

Dave laughed. 'She's not in the least like Kate. I mean she's got long dark hair . . .'

'That's just the point,' Susan broke in hurriedly. 'Kate had long dark hair before the baby was born.'

'Oh come off it, Julie; this is all too Freudian for me,' protested Dave with a wry grin.

The twilight had fallen while they had been discussing Mike, and no one had noticed. Susan stood up. 'I think we'd better make a move,' she said, reaching for her towel.

Julie looked awkwardly at them. 'Well, you'll come again soon?' she asked lightly.

'Of course,' Dave said. 'I enjoyed the psychology lecture.'

They all laughed, but an uncomfortable air of embarrassment still lingered as they said their goodbyes. Dave drove the car through the gates and Susan turned to smile and wave at Julie.

I wonder if there's any truth in what Julie says, she thought. If there is, then Kate must never know. She wouldn't, intentionally, have made Mike suffer. They were just good friends. Susan remembered Kate saying this herself.

She turned to Dave but his face was expressionless. 'Dave, you would never repeat what Julie said, would you?'

'What did she say?' he replied in a cool, neutral voice. 'I've forgotten already.'

'That's OK then,' muttered Susan. They drove

back in silence, and he dropped her off at the nurses' home.

'I've got to go back into hospital,' he said. 'Shall I see you tomorrow?'

'I expect so,' she said with a smile.

'No, I mean off duty.'

'Bit difficult . . . I think I'm a two-five tomorrow.'

How about Saturday—are you going to the concert?'

'Isn't everyone?' she asked. 'I'm dying to meet Mike's celebrity girlfriend.'

'Oh, she's quite something,' Dave said in an admiring tone.

I bet she is, thought Susan. Aloud she said, 'Well, I'll see you at the concert then.'

'I'll pick you up if you like.'

'That would be nice . . . thanks.'

Dave drove across the compound to park at the back of the hospital, and Susan climbed the staircase to her room. Out across the water she could see the twinkling lights of the cruise ship and hear the muffled sound of music and laughter.

CHAPTER FOUR

THE NEXT morning Susan found herself assigned to the breakfast feeding station. This time she was particularly careful to observe every woman and child she came in contact with. She tried to have a cheery word with each one. Some of them understood her, others simply gathered from the gentle voice that she was sympathetic towards them. Here was somebody they could trust.

The queue seemed longer than usual, and it was mid-morning before she was able to join her colleagues on the children's ward. Monica Hamlin was pleased to see her.

'Good to see you, Susan,' she said. 'Sister wants me to help her in Outpatients. I haven't started the dressings yet.'

'Have you made the list?' Susan asked.

'Yes, it's here on the desk.'

'OK. You go off to Outpatients and I'll deal with it.'

'Nurse Gusau is getting the trolley ready,' Monica said, smoothing back the unruly auburn curls under her little cap.

'Fine.' Susan's eyes scanned the dressings list. It looked as if it would take the rest of the morning. Methodically she organised it so that she started with the cleanest cases, going on to do the dirty wounds last.

Nurse Gusau opened the door from the sterilising room and pushed the trolley through. Susan went off to scrub up and gown, and they were soon working their way down the list. As they started on the burns cases the doors swung open and a tall fair-haired figure came down the ward.

Susan's pulse quickened, but she forced herself to concentrate on the patient in front of her. With skilful hands she continued to place the tulle gras expertly into position on the wound with her sterile forceps. She gave no indication that she knew those deep blue eyes were watching her. Straightening up, she asked in her most professional voice, 'Would you like to put the bandage on, Nurse Gusau?'

'Oh, yes please,' was the eager reply, as the young nurse stepped forward to take over.

'Was there something you wanted, Doctor?' Susan asked evenly as she lifted her eyes to his.

His steady gaze remained on her, the eyes cool and impersonal, as he said, 'Yes, Nurse. I've just been talking to Sister about my forthcoming trip into the bush. I have to visit the worst of the drought areas and I need to take a trained nurse with me.'

He seemed to pause deliberately, to watch her reaction. She gave no indication of her thoughts as she waited for him to continue.

'Sister suggested you. How would you feel about roughing it in the bush?'

He was actually smiling at her now . . . Oh, please keep on looking like that, she thought, as she gazed into the expressive blue eyes.

'I . . . I'm not sure,' she said quietly. 'It would be a challenge, but I'm sure I could manage.' She felt she could cope with the rigours of the tropical bush, but she wasn't sure about spending time alone with this unpredictable man . . .

'Good—that's settled then,' he said briskly. 'I'll brief you later—can't stop now, I'm needed in Outpatients.'

He turned and went out quickly, leaving Susan's thoughts in turmoil. There were so many questions she would like to have asked. When was this projected trip? Where exactly were they going? How long would they be away?

Nurse Gusau had finished the bandaging and was clearing away the dirty dressing. Susan pushed the trolley to the next small patient and scrubbed up. Nurse Gusau removed the outer dressings from Mbau's brown arms as he watched quietly. Susan noticed that healthy new skin was beginning to form at the edges of the wounds. Carefully taking a pair of forceps, she dipped a swab into the diluted antiseptic and cleaned the wounds before gently powdering with sulphona-mide and finally covering them.

'Tell Mbau I'm pleased with his progress,' she said to Nurse Gusau with a smile. The little boy smiled back when Nurse Gusau spoke to him.

'He's brave,' Susan said as they went on to the next patient.

She had been right about the dressings. It took her all morning to finish them, and then it was time to start feeds again.

After lunch, when it was time for her off duty, Susan felt tired. The hot climate and unaccustomed humidity were beginning to take their toll. She went to her bedroom and lay down, intending to read the new book she had started on the plane. The bookmark had fallen out during her unpacking, so she skimmed idly through the first few chapters. Before she had even found her place, the book had dropped from her hands on to the sheet and she was asleep.

It was still hot when she awoke, but through the open window Susan could see that the sun was lower in the sky. She glanced at her watch. Ten to five!

Heavens! I've slept all afternoon . . .

Her uniform was draped over a chair, where she had flung it after lunch. Hurriedly she stepped into it and raked a comb through her hair. She was still fixing her cap as she crossed the hospital compound, almost bumping into Dave Collins.

'Don't forget the concert,' he called breezily.

'I won't . . . can't stop now!'

She decided to take a short cut through Out-patients. Sister Obutu was tidying one of the inspection trolleys. 'Nurse Bradshaw, can I have a word?'

Susan stopped. 'Of course, Sister.'

Sister Obutu pushed the trolley back against the wall as Susan walked across into the cubicle. 'I'm glad you volunteered to go out to the field clinic, Nurse. It won't be easy, but it will be good experience for you.'

Susan stood rooted to the spot. Had she heard correctly? Volunteered? She didn't remember volunteering. Dr Gregson had said Sister had suggested her . . .

'Yes, I'm sure it will be good experience,' she found herself saying. Better not say any more. Supposing—but no, that was silly. The high and mighty doctor could have taken anyone he chose. All the nurses were his willing slaves. They all adored him and would happily go with him anywhere. He had chosen her because she needed the experience. Or perhaps no other nurse could be spared?

Sister was watching her carefully, unaware of her tangled thoughts. 'Is there any help you need in your preparations, Nurse?' she was saying.

'Well, I haven't really had time to think about it yet,' Susan said carefully. 'Dr Gregson said he would brief me . . .'

'Ah, well, there's no time like the present,' said Sister briskly. 'He's just finishing his last patient over here . . .'

'But they're waiting for me in Children's,' Susan protested.

'Oh, that's all right. Nurse Hamlin's in there. Let's get this expedition fixed first. Dr Gregson!' Sister called him as she pulled back the curtains of the end cubicle.

Susan held back, aware that Mike Gregson was none too pleased at the interruption. He lifted his eyes from the patient and looked steadily at her.

'Nurse Bradshaw was saying she'd like you to fill her in on the field clinic visit,' Sister said breezily, unaware of the tension she was creating.

The deep blue eyes flashed angrily as he pulled himself to his full height. 'I told Nurse I would brief her later,' he said in an ominously quiet voice.

'But I thought as you were nearly finished, Doctor,' countered Sister sweetly.

'You're right, Sister—I've *nearly* finished, but not quite,' he replied with studied calm. 'Perhaps Nurse Bradshaw would spare me a few minutes when she comes off duty tonight—say nine o'clock?'

He turned back to the patient, and Susan realised she had been dismissed. Sister shrugged her shoulders and smiled as she closed the curtains. As they stepped outside she whispered, 'He can be very difficult sometimes; don't worry, Nurse.'

'I'm not worrying, Sister,' Susan said firmly. 'Now, if you'll excuse me, I'd like to get back to the babies.'

Sister smiled. 'Of course, Nurse. I'll be along there soon.'

I wish she wouldn't interfere, Susan thought, and then immediately reprimanded herself for her unkind thoughts. I suppose she's just trying to help . . .

She had no time to think during the evening rush. It was almost nine o'clock before the last baby was settled down. Only then did she realise that Dr Gregson had given her no indication of where he would be for their rendezvous.

If he thinks I'm going to go chasing after him, she thought . . . The doors swung open, and there he was. Susan finished the sentence she was writing in the report book before putting her pen down and lifting her eyes to meet his.

He smiled at her, and she forgot his earlier brusqueness.

'I've almost finished,' she said quietly.

'Good.' He paused while his eyes scanned the room. 'Any chance of a cup of coffee? I'm parched.'

The man's human after all, she thought. 'I think that could be arranged,' she replied, leading the way across the ward, through the feeds kitchen into a small side ward where the nurses had an electric kettle and a jar of instant coffee.

'I hope you take it black, because we've no

milk,' she said as she switched on the kettle.

'Of course I take it black.' She knew he was smiling, even though her back was towards him. 'I've done so many treks into the bush, where milk is non-existent, that I stopped taking it a long time ago.'

She turned to face him. 'How long shall we be away?' she asked in a matter-of-fact tone of voice. Better not let him see how scared I am, she resolved.

'Oh, only a few days this time,' was the reassuring reply. 'We'll drive out to the field clinic at Funa in the north of Matala.'

Susan poured boiling water on to the instant coffee and handed him a cup. He took a sip before giving her a long piece of paper. 'Here is a list of things you should take with you. I take it you've got mosquito boots?'

She looked taken aback. 'No,' she said quietly. 'Am I supposed to have?'

'We *are* in the tropics you know,' he snapped irritably. 'See if Sister can lend you a pair, otherwise we'll have to borrow some in Funa.'

Susan stared fixedly at the paper, beginning to wish she had never agreed to go on this assignment.

'It's a rather ancient list,' he was saying in a gentler tone. 'For example, you won't need to take a hip-bath.'

'I should hope not,' she said with a laugh.

'It's not as ridiculous as it sounds,' he replied

quickly. 'When we trek into the bush, hip-baths are extremely welcome, I can tell you.'

Susan had a sudden vision of Mike Gregson's tall frame folded into a small hip-bath, and she smiled merrily.

'What's so funny?' he asked.

'Nothing, Doctor,' she assured him hastily.

'Why not call me Mike?' he said suddenly, and she had that same weak feeling in her legs. She dare not look into those deep blue eyes. The sudden feeble cry of one of the babies from the ward reminded her that she still had to give the report to the night staff. Quickly she drained her cup and stood up. It was a very small room and Mike was standing very close to her—too close for comfort. She edged towards the door.

'So you'll be ready for Monday?' he was saying in a brisk, no-nonsense voice.

'Yes, I'll be ready . . . I've got to give the report.' She excused herself quickly and hurried back into the ward.

In the next couple of days Susan found all her off-duty time taken up with preparations for the trip to Funa. Sister Obutu proved a great help in lending equipment. She managed to find a pair of mosquito boots for Susan to wear, and they both laughed as she tried them on.

'Not very elegant are they, Sister?' Susan grinned, parading round the sitting-room in the nurses' home in the heavy knee-length black leather boots.

'No, but you'll definitely need them in the evenings. Mosquito bites can be very nasty, so don't be tempted to go out without them,' Sister said. 'Are you going to the concert tonight?'

'Yes—you're not suggesting I wear them, are you, Sister?'

'No,' Sister said, with a broad smile. 'I don't think you'll find mosquitoes in the air-conditioned hall of the Matala Broadcasting Corporation. Have you got a lift?'

'Yes—Dr Collins is taking me.'

'That's nice.' Sister Obutu's dark brown eyes were twinkling merrily. 'He's a very nice young man—easy to get on with.'

'Yes, he seems very pleasant . . . Well, thanks for your help, Sister—shall I see you at the concert?'

'If I can get off on time—I've got a ticket; nine o'clock start, isn't it? I'll see what I can do.'

It certainly seemed as if the entire hospital would be there, apart from the night staff. She must be quite a strong personality, this girlfriend of Mike Gregson, to organise such a big event, thought Susan. She found herself looking forward to the evening with something more than anticipation.

Dave picked her up at eight-thirty and they drove along the marina. The car windows were down and the circulating air was still hot. A million stars stared down at them and the warm gold of the moon danced on the water.

'You're looking very charming tonight, Susan.' Dave took his eyes briefly from the road ahead and Susan recognised his look of admiration.

'Thank you,' she said simply, feeling pleased that she had lashed out on this white lurex sheath dress before leaving London. It was too hot to wear tights, but her legs were beginning to turn to honey brown colour from their brief exposure to the tropical sun.

Dave drove through the still busy streets of Kyruba until they came to a tall grey stone building set back from the road.

'Here we are,' he said, driving into the large car park at the side. 'The MBC.'

Susan climbed out and looked around her. The car park was filling up quickly, and she recognized some of the hospital staff getting out of their cars. Dave locked the doors, put the keys in his pocket, and gently took hold of her arm. As he steered her towards the large impressive doorway at the front, Susan was vaguely aware of admiring glances. Dave looked a little self-conscious in his dinner jacket and bow-tie, but she was pleased to be seen with him. He was an attentive escort.

They went through the revolving doors of the MBC and into the crowded foyer. It was almost impossible to move in the crush, but little by little they edged their way through to the auditorium. Standing by the doors, waiting to greet everyone, was the hostess, Janice Morgan. Susan recognised the tall, striking figure with long dark hair, even though they had never met. Her long, superbly-manicured hands were reaching out to shake hands with everyone as she uttered the required greetings in a low, husky voice.

'*So* glad you could come—*lovely* to see you . . . Dave!' A touch of real warmth had come into the bored voice as she flashed green eyes provocatively at Dave.

'Darling, this is a surprise! I didn't know you were coming.'

'I wasn't sure if I could make it,' Dave said.

'I expect your chief works you terribly hard,' Janice said, glancing over her shoulder at Mike Gregson who was hovering nearby.

'What's that, darling?' Mike asked laughingly.

'Nothing, my love.' Janice blew him a kiss and continued to play the perfect hostess.

Behind her Mike was gazing across at Susan and Dave. He moved forwards and stood in front of them, looking devastatingly handsome. The expensive cut of the dark suit moulded around the lines of his athletic figure, showing it off to perfection.

Susan drew in her breath. His blue eyes were watching her impassively.

'Janice, I'd like you to meet Susan,' he said quietly. 'Susan is one of our new recruits at the hospital.'

'Delighted to meet you, my dear,' replied

Janice, stretching out a hand with impeccable long finger nails. In spite of the heat, it felt cold and clammy as Susan touched it briefly. 'A new recruit, eh? I didn't know novices were allowed out here. I thought you had to be trained or something . . .'

'Oh, Susan is a trained nurse . . .' Dave started to say, but Janice was no longer listening. With a toss of her long dark hair she had turned her attention on a tall, important-looking man, his hair greying slightly at the temples.

'Darling! How lovely to see you . . .' she was saying.

Susan felt Dave's hand on her arm, easing her throught the crowd, away from Janice and Mike.

What a well-matched pair, thought Susan bitterly. They deserve each other!

She willingly allowed herself to be shown to her seat in the auditorium. She could feel that Mike was watching her, but she didn't turn round.

When everyone was seated, the lights were dimmed and the excited babble of voices died away. A single spotlight shone, and a radiant Janice Morgan came through the curtains, centre-stage, to a burst of wild applause. The low-cut black dress showed off her sun-tan, and diamonds sparkled at her throat.

'Thank you . . . thank you, my *dear* friends,' she began, when it was possible to make herself heard. 'It's wonderful to see you all tonight.

Without your generosity this show would not have been possible . . .'

She went on to outline the need for more money in the campaign against the famine in the north, stressing the fact that all the proceeds from the concert were going to the relief fund. When she finished there was more tumultuous applause, from which Janice seemed to have difficulty in tearing herself away.

'She certainly enjoys the limelight,' whispered Dave.

'Don't be so uncharitable,' muttered Susan with a grin as she settled back to enjoy the first performer. Apparently the comedian now on the stage was quite well-known, but Susan, not being too well up on light entertainment, had never heard of him. She found his act fairly amusing, however, and noticed that Dave thought it hilarious. She recognised some of the artists later in the show, and the first half was enjoyable. From a commercial point of view it was an obvious success.

They all went out to the foyer at the interval. There was a scramble to get to the bar, but Dave had hurried out first and was waving a glass at Susan when she managed to push her way through.

'I hope you like gin and tonic,' he said amiably.'I had to make a quick decision before the crowd arrived.'

'That's fine, thank you,' said Susan, sinking

down on to a chair beside the last remaining
table. Dave stood beside her and they sipped
their drinks. Above the noise in the bar, Susan
heard a high-pitched bleep.

'Oh no,' said Dave, feeling for the bleeper in
his pocket. 'I'll have to get to a phone and see
who wants me. I'm on call at the hospital.'

He put his drink down on the table and went
back to the bar.

'Is there a phone I can use?' he asked one of
the stewards. 'I'm a doctor, and . . .'

'Through here, sir,' the steward said helpfully.

Dave disappeared behind the bar through a
door. Susan felt very lonely after he had gone.
She looked across the crowded room and saw
Janice and Mike entertaining a huge crowd of
friends. The champagne corks were popping . . .

'Susan.' Dave was back, looking anxiously at
her. 'I've got to go back to the hospital—will you
be OK?'

'Yes, of course—I'll take a taxi,' she said
quickly.

'Must dash. Bye.' And he was gone.

She sipped her drink, feeling terribly out of it.
She was glad when the bell went at the end of the
interval. The second half seemed to drag on. It
wasn't Susan's kind of show and she felt bored.
There were too many short acts. Just as she
began to feel a glimmer of interest the act
finished and someone else rushed on.

Oh well, it's all for a good cause, she thought as

the final curtain came down. Without Dave to help her it was difficult to battle a way through the throng in the foyer. No one was in a hurry to move, and people were simply standing around chatting. Eventually Susan found herself out on the front steps. She looked around for a taxi. Surely there would be taxis available after such an important concert?

For several minutes she stood waiting on the steps without success. Perhaps I'd better phone for a taxi, she thought, and turned to get back inside, almost colliding with a tall, fair-haired figure as she did so.

'I'm terribly sorry . . .' she began, and then broke off. 'Oh . . . Dr Gregson—I mean, Mike.'

He seemed amused at her discomfort.

'All alone, Susan?' he asked in a gentle tone.

'Yes . . . Dave's been called back, so I was hoping to get a taxi.'

'This is Kyruba, not London. You'll be lucky to get a taxi without booking one,' he said, not unkindly. 'I can give you a lift back, if you like.'

'That's very good of you,' she said quickly. 'But what about your, er . . .'

'Janice? She's having a big party. It'll go on all night, and I've got to be up early, so I've cried off.'

As she felt his hand under her arm, Susan stiffened—but he gave no indication that he had noticed her apprehension as they walked together into the car park towards his car. It was a long, low, expensive-looking sports car. What else? she thought as he opened the door for her to climb in. A little boy had been guarding the car and he beamed happily when Mike tossed him a coin and said something in Matalan.

'Thank you, sir, thank you,' replied the boy, as he clutched the coin.

Mike climbed in beside Susan and turned the ignition key. The powerful car burst into action and they drove out of the car park, along the narrow streets to the marina. Half-way along, Mike suddenly pulled the car off the road and into a clearing in the pine trees, looking out across the water. He switched off the engine and turned to look at her in the moonlight.

With difficulty Susan forced herself to gaze into those deep blue, searching eyes.

'I'm sorry if Janice seemed rude tonight,' he said gently. 'It was my fault for calling you a new recruit.'

'That's all right,' said Susan, amazed at the change in his manner.

There was an awkward silence and then he went on lightly, 'Are you ready for our trek to the north?'

'Yes; Sister Obutu has been very helpful,' she said quickly. 'I've got some mosquito boots.'

He laughed boyishly. 'I'm glad about that, Susan.' There was something about the way he said her name . . .

She turned away from those piercing eyes and

looked out across the water. Why was it that she wanted this moment to last? It wasn't as if she even liked this man. He was arrogant, difficult, unpredictable—and anyway, he had a celebrity girlfriend. No one could possibly compete with the fantastic Janice . . . even if they wanted to.

Her heart turned over as she heard him start up the engine again. She experienced an emotion not unlike disappointment as the strong sensitive hands turned the wheel and headed back on to the marina road.

Neither of them spoke as he drove towards the hospital. The car came to a halt and Susan tried to open the door at once, but it was the kind of handle she wasn't used to. Clumsily she fiddled with it until, looking up, she saw that Mike had come round to help her.

'Allow me,' he said, deftly opening the door.

Furious with herself, she stepped out. 'Thanks,' she said ungraciously. He smiled, and his eyes had a far-away look.

'Good night,' he murmured softly, and stooped to brush her cheek with a kiss. His warm lips were fleetingly upon her skin, and she looked up in amazement—but he had already turned and was hurrying away.

Susan rubbed her cheek, the place where he had kissed her. She felt weak and trembly as she crossed to the nurses' home. I mustn't read too much into a mere kiss on the cheek, she told herself. Mike mixes with Janice's show-biz friends, and they're always kissing each other. He just forgot it was me . . . he had a far-away look in his eyes.

She closed her bedroom door and lay down on the bed, looking out at the lights twinkling on the harbour. Had she glimpsed the old Mike Gregson—the one Kate used to describe in her letters? Perhaps . . . But it wouldn't last— she had seen him too often in an arrogant mood which made it perfectly clear that he disliked her. Well, the feeling was mutual. She had no time to worry about him. One thing she was quite sure about. Their relationship on the expedition to Funa would be solely professional.

CHAPTER FIVE

THE EXPEDITION to the Funa clinic started out early in the morning, while it was still relatively cool. Mike had said he wanted to arrive at their destination by late afternoon, before darkness fell, and although it was only about one hundred and twenty miles there was some difficult terrain to cover. Susan sat at his side as the heavy Land-Rover drove through the streets of Kyruba and turned north. She was still drowsy from her sleep and appreciated the fact that Mike, too, had no desire to talk.

The road ran in a straight line between shanty huts for a few miles, to the village of Nagow, where small brown children waved to them as they walked to the mission school, carrying incongruous-looking satchels on their thin shoulders. Occasionally Susan saw someone selling bright green oranges or long stems of bananas at the side of the road.

Beyond Nagow the road curved tortuously through the bush and lost all appearance of civilisation. No attempt had been made to improve its surface, which varied continually, according to the whim of the seasons. It was now dry and dusty, the red laterite puffing out clouds

79

behind them, like a smoke-screen. As Susan turned to look back down the road she could see nothing except red dust hanging in the air. Mike was concentrating all his attention on negotiating the pot-holes in the road. They seemed to be travelling at a snail's pace. Susan began to doubt if they would ever get there. She felt hot and thirsty long before Mike stopped for their mid-day break.

The Land-Rover lurched to a halt at the side of what had obviously been a wide river, but was now dried up to a small trickle of brackish water.

'I don't think we'll have any problem crossing the ford,' said Mike with a wry grin. It was the first thing he had said for several miles, and Susan felt relieved that he had broken the rather strained silence.

'Shall I get the food out?' she asked nervous-ly. It had been her job to arrange the rations with the hospital kitchen, and she was begin-ning to have doubts about what had been packed.

Mike leaned back in his seat and ran a hand through his fair hair.

'That would be a good idea,' he said amiably. 'I'm starving—what have you brought?'

'I'll show you, if you'll hold on a minute . . . Where are we going to eat this?' she said, reaching into the back of the Land-Rover.

'Well, obviously we can't have a picnic on the grass,' he said drily. 'There's no grass, and we'd get bitten to death by the insects if we ventured to sit on the ground.'

'I thought about that,' said Susan quietly. 'So I've brought a table.'

'A table?' Mike laughed.

'It's only a small picnic table—and a couple of camp stools,' she said defensively as she started to unload.

'Here, let me give you a hand,' he offered as he swung himself down on to the roadside. 'I must say I'm impressed at your ingenuity, Susan.'

'Thanks,' she said, smiling inwardly.

'In all the time I've been trekking out here, I've never had a picnic before. We'd better put this table under those trees, or we shall fry ourselves.' He lifted the table and stools and carried them over to a clump of withered bushes, while Susan followed with a wicker basket.

Sinking down on to one of the stools, he watched her through veiled lashes as she set out the food on the table. She had persuaded the cook to lend her an iced carrying box so there was butter to go with the thick crusty bread, and ice-cold beer.

Mike pulled the ring off his can and drank thirstily. 'That's better,' he smiled as he put the can back on the table. 'I needed that. This dust gets everywhere.'

Susan produced a cold chicken and some salad from the box, followed by iced paw-paw.

'Wonders never cease,' Mike said as he finished the last of the refreshing fruit. 'I must say I feel a lot better. Well done.'

She smiled happily at his praise, taking a side-long glance at him. Yes, he could be quite pleasant when he wanted to. She dropped her eyes towards the sun-baked earth when he saw her looking at him.

'Look, Mike!' she cried in amazement. 'Look at that piece of bread.'

A small piece of bread had fallen to the floor and an army of ants had descended upon it. The front column carried it off, holding it high above the ground, followed by the rear guard in a long, narrow formation.

'Such organisation,' marvelled Susan. 'It's difficult to imagine how tiny creatures can be so clever.'

As she watched the long column busy its way out of sight among the trees, she forgot about her companion. She forgot her determination to keep a professional relationship. Flushed with excitement she turned towards Mike, and saw that he had been watching her closely, a tender look in those deep blue eyes.

Embarrassed, she sprang to her feet and started to tidy away the picnic. When she looked again, Mike was loading the Land-Rover, a cool, impersonal look on his face.

'Would you like me to drive?' she asked when everything was stowed away.

He laughed. 'No, I don't think you'd better,' he said dismissively.

'I'm a very good driver,' she retorted.

'I'm sure you are—under normal conditions. But you haven't seen anything yet. Just wait until we get going along the next stretch.'

Susan resented his patronising tone. She climbed back into the truck without saying another word.

Mike let in the clutch and rolled the Land-Rover forwards through the dried mud to the river bed. The tyres crunched their way over the baked earth, and Susan found herself bouncing up and down in her seat. She reached for the seat-belt, but even as she did so, an extra-strong jolt threw her upwards to hit her head on the roof of the vehicle.

An automatic cry of pain issued from her lips. Instinctively Mike braked and stopped the motor.

'For heaven's sake, woman, put your seat-belt on!' he cried. His blue eyes were flashing angrily as he turned to look at her. She was crouched miserably in her seat, with a hand tentatively exploring the place on her forehead where a thin trickle of blood issued from the skin.

'Susan—oh, Susan, I'm sorry.' The cold expression in his eyes had changed to one of concern.

'I'm OK. It's nothing—I should have put my seat-belt on before we started . . .' she was muttering. Her pride was wounded more than her head.

'Yes, you should,' he said quietly. 'But we'd better do something about that cut.'

He reached in the back for the first-aid box and took out the antiseptic and some cotton swabs.

'Here, let me have a look at it,' he said in a cool, professional voice.

Mortified, Susan turned towards him as his skilful hands stemmed the flow of blood before applying a dressing, covered by a plaster.

'Not as bad as I thought,' he said, surveying his handiwork.

She could feel his warm breath upon her face as he examined her forehead, and she felt shivers run down her spine.

'You'll have a nasty bruise,' he said quietly.

'Well, I'll just have to cancel all my social engagements in Funa for the next few days,' she said flippantly.

Mike laughed. 'Yes, I think you should,' he agreed. His arm was resting gently on the back of her seat, but he took it away and put it back on the wheel.

'Let's go—it's still a long way.'

The afternoon wore on, the sun still high in the sky. Susan found herself longing for the cool of the twilight. Would that great big sun ever stop blazing down on them? Mile after mile of un-dulating track stretched ahead of them, and by the time they reached Funa they were both exhausted.

The sun had started its slow descent as they drove into the medical compound. Susan had expected it to be primitive, but it was even more underdeveloped than she had imagined. The clinic consisted of a group of wattle and bamboo huts grouped around a single water pump. A dark-skinned health worker wearing a white coat came to meet them, a broad smile on her friendly face.

'Welcome to Funa,' she called as Mike pulled the Land-Rover to a halt. 'Did you have a good journey, Doctor?'

Mike grinned. 'The usual,' he replied. 'But we're dying for a drink, Ladi.'

'Of course, Doctor.' She looked shyly at Susan, waiting for an introduction.

'Oh, this is Nurse Bradshaw. She's come out to help me,' Mike said.

Ladi smiled, displaying strong white teeth in the dark face. 'Come with me, Dr Gregson—and Nurse, too.' She led them into one of the larger huts, which was surprisingly cool. The bamboo roof had filtered away the warmth of the sun and the thick wattle walls also helped to keep out the heat. They sat on wooden stools, grouped round a table on which Ladi placed glasses and a jug of water.

Mike looked enquiringly at the jug of water, and she interpreted his glance. 'Don't worry,

Doctor; I've got something stronger for you.'

'I'm glad about that,' said Mike as he pushed the fair hair back from his damp forehead.

Ladi produced a bottle of whisky and poured some into a glass. She turned to Susan. 'Nurse Bradshaw?'

Mike answered for her.

'I think Nurse should have a stiff drink too—it's been a long day.'

'Thank you, Ladi,' Susan said, as the health worker poured whisky into her glass. She raised it to her lips and sipped gently. Soon the strong liquid seemed to send a warm glow through her body. She relaxed as she put the glass down on the table.

'Well, how have things been since I was last here?' asked Mike.

'Pretty much the same, Doctor—we struggle on. The drought doesn't get any easier and we've got a measles epidemic at the moment.'

'Measles?' Susan's interest was immediately roused. So that's where the two cases had come from.

'Yes,' said Ladi. 'Our main concern is the complication of respiratory problems. And, of course, we haven't room to nurse them all here. I try to get round the worst cases but it's an uphill battle.'

'You need more help, Ladi,' said Mike. 'I'll see if I can send you some more nurses from Kyruba.'

'Thank you, Doctor,' she said quietly. 'But they never want to stay out here—the conditions are too primitive. I was born out here so I can survive, but most nurses who come here don't want to stay . . .'

'Then we'll have to train more health workers from the Kulani tribe,' said Mike earnestly. 'Do you think you could organise that, Ladi?'

'I have already started to take volunteers, but it is hard work,' she admitted with a gentle smile. 'Many are afraid of the white man's medicine,' she added simply.

'I've brought you the supplies you asked for,' Mike said.

'Oh, thank you, Doctor.' She turned to look at Susan. 'Would you like me to show you to your quarters, Nurse?'

'Yes please, Ladi. Any chance of a shower?'

Mike laughed. 'You must be joking. Water is strictly rationed here.'

'I can arrange a hip-bath for Nurse Bradshaw,' Ladi said quickly.

Susan flashed her a grateful smile. 'That would be marvellous.'

'Come this way,' Ladi murmured in her soft Matalan accent.

Susan stood up and followed her outside the hut. The sun was now low in the sky. Soon it would be twilight, and then darkness. Already the mosquitoes were beginning to hang in the air.

'Better hurry,' Ladi said. 'You must finish your bath before nightfall.'

She led the way across the dry compound to a small hut on the perimeter. Inside, a young girl was sitting on a rush mat beside the narrow camp-bed. A tough mosquito net had been hung from a wooden canopy over the bed and tucked into the sides. Through the net, Susan could see that the bed had already been made up with cool white cotton sheets. She was tempted to forego the bath and crawl between them, but Ladi had already started to put things in motion.

The young girl was listening intently to the instructions, nodding in aquiescence, a friendly smile lighting up her dark face. When Ladi had finished speaking, she disappeared outside the hut to collect the necessities for the bathing operation.

'That's Binta,' said Ladi, when the girl had gone. 'She will look after you during your stay here. Her English is limited, I'm afraid, but she's very willing to learn. I think she's intelligent enough to be trained as a health worker when she's a little older.'

'How old is she?' asked Susan, sitting down on a small stool and surveying her new quarters.

'About thirteen or fourteen,' said Ladi vaguely.

Susan looked round the hut. It was sparsely furnished, but in spite of its simplicity she felt it would be adequate for a few days—but no longer!

Binta returned carrying a small hip-bath. Behind her, hovering in the doorway, was a young Kulani boy, grinning shyly. He was carrying a bucket of water.

'Come in, Fudayin,' said Ladi. Still the young boy hung back, afraid to enter.

Ladi spoke gently to him in his own language. As Binta placed the hip-bath in the centre of the hut, he stepped forward, tipped the contents of the bucket into it and hurriedly retreated, without looking at Susan.

'When you have finished your bath, call for Binta and Fudayin,' said Ladi. 'They will be waiting outside.'

Well I'm glad about that, thought Susan . . . What a performance!

She waited for Binta and Ladi to go out before firmly closing the rough wooden door. There was a small space at the top which allowed the daylight to filter in. Better not light the lamp—it would only attract the mosquitoes.

Susan peeled off her clothes and flung them on to a stool before stepping into the small bath. The water was tepid, having been standing in the bucket in the sunshine. She remembered Mike telling her that a hip-bath would be welcome in the bush—how right he was! It felt luxurious to bathe her sticky skin, and although her knees were tucked up to her chin, she began to feel relaxed and refreshed. She dried herself on the towel, surprised to find how soft, clean and fluffy it was. Evidently they still had some sort of laundry arrangements even in the drought—or was she being given VIP treatment?

Someone had already placed her travel bag in the hut, so she pulled out a pale blue long-sleeved shirt, white cotton trousers and Sister Obutu's mosquito boots. She dressed slowly, feeling strangely lethargic at the end of her long day. It seemed odd to be pulling on knee-length boots in this heat, but she'd better not take any chances. Already Susan could see a couple of mosquitoes sitting on the outside of the net, waiting to pounce if anyone was foolish enough to let them inside. She combed her hair, trying to get a full-length glimpse of herself in her small hand mirror. It was impossible so she gave up. Anyway, who would see her out there? Only Mike, and he wouldn't notice. He seemed to prefer the sophisticated, well-groomed type of woman, if Janice was anything to go by—cold, unemotional, and beautiful to look at.

She stepped outside the hut and found Binta and Fudayin waiting patiently. They were about the same age, Susan decided . . . Binta slightly more developed, and not so shy as Fudayin.

'I've finished my bath,' she said obviously.

Binta smiled. 'Bath finish,' she repeated, proud to display her linguistic prowess.

'Yes . . . thank you,' Susan said, and watched

as Binta and Fudayin carried out the bath between them and emptied it over a small plot of earth nearby, where an attempt to grow yams was being made. Obviously no one ever wasted a drop of precious water.

She walked across the compound in the gathering twilight to the hut where Ladi had first taken them.

Mike was sitting outside, puffing on a cigar. He had changed into a khaki safari suit, and the tension of the day had left him. The blue eyes watched appraisingly as she approached.

'How was the bath?' he asked with a friendly grin.

'Sheer luxury!'

'I can imagine. Come and sit down, Susan. Do you want a cigar?' he asked in a neutral voice, as if it were perfectly natural.

'Good heavens, no! I don't smoke—and I certainly couldn't manage a cigar,' she said with a laugh.

'I don't smoke either, except out here. It helps to keep the mosquitoes away, so I always bring a packet with me.'

'Well, just puff some smoke this way then,' she suggested. He drew deeply on his cigar and blew a smoke ring around her hair.

'There—that should give you some immunity for a few minutes. Are you hungry? I think Ladi is organising some food for us.'

'Now you mention it, I am—starving, in fact,'

she admitted. 'I wonder what's on the menu.'

Mike smiled. 'I should imagine it's chicken,' he said, pointing to a couple of scrawny-looking birds pecking hopefully nearby. 'It usually is. Have you had West African chicken?'

'Not yet,' she replied.

'It's an acquired taste. Not everyone likes it, but out here we've no choice. I can smell its delicious aroma—let's go.' He stood up, stubbing out his cigar in the dusty earth, then pushing it well in with the sole of his mosquito boot.

Susan watched. 'You looked as if you're trying to plant it,' she said with an amused smile.

'That would be a good idea.' He grinned mischievously. 'A cigar plantation.'

They both laughed and the ice was well and truly broken. He took her arm and led her across to the cookhouse. She felt relaxed and happy. Mike was so good to be with when he was like this. The feel of his hand on her arm sent shivers of tingling sensations down into her fingers.

Ladi came forward to greet them as they went into the cookhouse. It was larger than the other huts and a lamp had been lit inside, sending a cosy glow around the walls. The door and windows had been carefully sealed off with wire mesh to keep out the mosquitoes.

'Sit down here, Doctor,' she said, pointing to a stool by a wooden table. 'And here, Nurse.'

Susan sat in the place indicated, across the table from Mike, and Ladi sat beside her.

Tunde, the Kulani cook, came over from the stove carrying bowls of steaming soup, which he placed in front of them. Susan picked up her spoon and started to eat.

'Mm, that's good,' she said. 'What is it, Ladi?'

'Yams,' she replied simply.

'Yams are rather like potatoes,' explained Mike. 'They're much harder though—you have to cook them longer than potatoes, but they're very tasty.'

'Especially if you're as hungry as I am,' Susan smiled as she finished the bowl.

Ladi took the bowls away and returned with a small roast chicken on a plate. 'I hope there's enough,' she said doubtfully as she placed it on the table.

'That looks big enough to me,' Mike said helpfully, picking up a large carving knife from the table.

The chicken proved to be extremely tough both to cut and then to eat. Mike had difficulty in sharing it out between the three of them, but he smiled at Ladi to put her at her ease.

'I think it's marvellous the way you can produce a meal like this out here,' he commented as he struggled to cut a particularly stubborn piece of chicken.

Ladi smiled gently, obviously pleased at his praise. When the more edible parts of the chicken had been consumed, she left the table to return with some oranges. They, like the

chicken, were tough, but Susan found what
little juice they had was sweet and refreshing.

'Take your coffee outside,' Ladi said. 'I must
leave you now—I have to go round the patients.'

Mike stood up. 'I'd like to come with you,
Ladi.'

She looked alarmed. 'Not tonight, Doctor. My
nurses are not expecting you until tomorrow—
they are not prepared.'

He laughed. 'I hope they're not going to roll
out the red carpet for me.'

Ladi looked puzzled. 'I will take you round in
the morning, sir,' she said quietly. 'Good night
Doctor, good night Nurse.'

The cook had placed two cups of black coffee
on the table, so Mike and Susan picked them up
and went outside. The tropical night had fallen
quickly while they were having their meal. The
moon had risen high in the sky, casting a bright,
eerie glow over the medical compound. It was
silent except for the droning and clicking of the
insects in the dry bushes. They sat down on a
wooden bench, which someone had placed outside the cookhouse.

Susan sipped her coffee. Out of the corner of
her eye she could see Mike lighting a cigar. As he
struck a match his face was illuminated in the
glow. She saw the deep blue of those expressive
eyes and her heart gave a leap of recognition.
What had Kate said about the signs and symptoms of love? You'll recognise them when they

come . . . No, no, I can't—I mustn't fall in love with this man. He's too unpredictable . . . He's wonderful when he's relaxed and fun-loving like this, but it won't last. And anyway, there's Janice to contend with . . .

'What are you thinking, Susan?' The blue eyes held hers for a brief moment before she looked away.

'Nothing,' she said quickly. 'I was just thinking how peaceful it is.' They sat in companionable silence for a few minutes before she stood up.

'I'm going to turn in, Mike,' she said. 'I expect we shall have to be up early tomorrow.'

'Yes, we rise with the sun out here,' he told her gently. 'To make the most of the daylight.' He stood up and looked down at her in the moon-light. Suddenly he reached forward, as if on impulse, and put his hands on the top of her arms. She could feel his strong fingers through the flimsy cotton of her shirt. In a daze of anti-cipation she raised her eyes. His expression held a far-away look of tenderness, which she had never seen before. For one brief moment she thought he was going to kiss her but, quickly as it came, the moment vanished. The expressive eyes took on a cold, neutral look, and his arms dropped to his sides. He gave a sigh of resignation and turned away.

'Good night, Susan,' he said quietly, and strode off across the compound.

She stood rooted to the spot, watching that

tall, masculine frame vanishing in the moonlight. Oh, how embarrassing . . . Did he know the effect he had on her? How could she be so stupid? It was a silly infatuation she was feeling. But oh, Mike . . . If only . . .

She shook herself briskly and walked over to her sleeping quarters. Carefully she bolted the wooden door. Binta must have been in to tidy up and light the lamp. A mesh grid had been placed over the window, but even so, Susan could hear the high-pitched hum of a lone mosquito. She felt too tired to try and catch it as it hovered in the air. I'll just tuck my net in very carefully, she thought. Undressing quickly, she turned out the lamp and crept into bed, making sure that the net was tucked in around her. Almost as soon as her head touched the pillow she fell asleep.

In her dreams there was a man—and this time she recognised him at once. The tender expression in those deep blue eyes—she knew where she had seen it. The fair, unruly hair, flopping over his forehead; the mischievous grin on those sensuous lips . . .

She awoke with a start. The moonlight was streaming into the hut. She could hear the sounds of the tropical night, but she felt safe and secure, cocooned in her little bed, protected by the mosquito net. Nothing—and no one—could touch her in here . . .

CHAPTER SIX

WHEN SUSAN awoke again it was daylight outside. The warmth of the tropical sun was already
making itself felt. She dressed carefully in the
white uniform she had brought with her and went
outside. Binta was sitting on the ground in the
early-morning sun, looking relaxed and carefree.
She jumped up when she saw Susan.

'Good morning, Binta,' Susan said with a
friendly smile.

'Morning,' Binta said shyly. 'I go make bed.'

'Thank you, Binta.'

Susan crossed the compound towards the
cookhouse. A long-tailed lizard scurried across
her path, its bright red head gleaming in the
sunlight and a couple of chickens were pecking in
the dust.

She could smell coffee as she went into the
round hut. Tunde gave her a welcoming smile
and handed her a mug of strong black coffee,
motioning for her to sit down at the table. As she
did so, Mike came through the doorway. He
greeted her with a brief, 'Good morning,' as he
sat down, but he seemed lost in thought, hardly
noticing she was there. It was as if nothing
had happened last night—well, nothing did

happen, thought Susan ruefully. The most romantic thing was my dream. I must stop imagining things . . .

She turned to Mike and said, 'Did you sleep well?'

He paused as he sipped his coffee and looked at her, a cool expression in his liquid blue eyes. He seemed surprised at her familiarity. It was as if he'd never seen her before.

'Yes, thank you, and I hope *you* did, because we've got a lot of work to do today,' he replied briskly.

'Oh, I'm feeling very fit—don't worry.' I knew it was too good to last, she thought. Thank goodness I didn't make a fool of myself last night.

Tunde was placing a dark, crusty loaf on the table and one of the jars of marmalade they had brought with them. Susan looked across at the primitive stove. Yes, it would be too difficult to make toast on a weird contraption like that. She resigned herself to cutting off a small section of bread and spreading it generously with marmalade.

Their frugal breakfast barely finished, Mike leapt to his feet and said tersely, 'I think we should make a move, Nurse.'

My, we are formal again, thought Susan as she obediently stood up and followed her boss outside. The bright sunlight dazzled her eyes after the gloomy interior of the cookhouse. She put a hand up to shield them and paused momentarily.

Mike turned round impatiently. 'Oh, for good-ness' sake, Nurse, hurry up.'

She swallowed her pride and quickened her pace to catch up with the long strides of the doctor. He was making for a low wooden build-ing at the edge of the compound. This, apparent-ly, was the main clinic. A couple of auxiliary Matalan nurses were standing outside, dispens-ing a thin gruel mixture to a straggling queue of Kulanis. Mike spoke briefly to the nurses, who nodded and smiled at Susan.

This is obviously some form of introduction, thought Susan, as she returned their smile.

She followed Mike into the long wooden hut. It was incredibly hot; she wanted to fling wide the windows, but saw that they were covered with wire mesh to keep out the flies and mosquitoes. Ladi was half-way down the hut, bending over an emaciated old woman. She spoke gently to her patient before straightening up and walking down between the rows of narrow beds to greet Mike and Susan.

Her gentle brown face wore a smile of wel-come. 'Would you like me to take you round?'

'Yes, of course, Ladi.' Mike was cool and impersonal. He was wearing his white hospital coat, his stethoscope slung round his neck, and looked ready for action.

Ladi took them round the adult section of the hut, where the patients were mostly suffering from malnutrition or diseases exacerbated by malnourishment. In the next section were the children and babies, many accompanied by their mothers.

'We encourage the mothers to stay with their children,' Ladi said. 'Apart from anything else, they are very useful as helpers. We simply haven't enough nurses to look after them, and it's a great comfort to know that a child is being constantly supervised by its own mother. As you see, they are quite happy to sleep on a mat by the side of their children.'

She led the way through to the final section. As they went through the narrow wooden door, a young Matalan nurse stepped forward quietly and handed each of them a white gown.

'This is our isolation unit,' Ladi explained. 'I have to keep a nurse on the door, otherwise people would wander in and out. At the moment it's strictly for our measles patients. We bring the worst cases in, but the others have to remain outside, with their families.'

Susan cast her eyes around the cots and beds, and was alarmed to see the number of children with respiratory complications. Mike, too, seemed moved by the sight of the tiny, under-nourished mites, struggling for breath.

'Let's take each case one by one, Ladi,' he said as he bent down over the first bed.

The tiny little dusky-faced boy was about ten years old, but looked much younger. He was lying flat on the mattress, staring up at them out of watery eyes. Susan could hear the sterterous and difficult sounds of his breathing.

'Do we have any more pillows anywhere?' she asked, leaning forward to raise the small patient upright. She supported the thin, bony frame with her arm until Ladi brought her a couple of pillows and helped to prop the boy up.

'There, that's better,' Susan said. 'He should breathe easier like that.'

Mike pressed his stethoscope to the young boy's chest and listened intently, before peering down his throat. As he straightened up he said quietly, 'Is he on antibiotics?'

'No, Doctor.'

'I think he'd better have some.' Mike picked up the chart at the foot of the bed. 'I don't like the sound of that chest, and the larynx is inflamed. Can you spare a nurse to special him, Ladi?'

'Not really,' began Ladi, but Susan interrupted quickly.

'I could special, if you like.'

Mike's eyes narrowed thoughtfully as he looked at her. 'I don't see why not,' he said.

'I can help with the other patients in here, when I'm needed,' Susan hurried on.

'Thank you, Nurse.' Mike's voice was coolly professional, but he seemed relieved as he and Ladi moved on to the next patient.

Susan rolled up the sleeves of her gown. The first thing she wanted to do was sponge down her small patient. He was hot and feverish and looked desperately uncomfortable.

She found a water jug at the side of the unit and poured some into a bowl. Gently she swabbed the febrile skin and patted it dry. As she worked she talked quietly to the little boy, using the smattering of Matalan that she had picked up. She didn't learn much from him except that his name was Shehu. When he was propped back on his pillows, in a more comfortable position, Susan went off in search of some penicillin. One of the nurses directed her to a room at the end of the unit, where a small supply of drugs was kept.

No good trying to give him anything by mouth, she thought, as she carefully drew up the required dose of penicillin into a syringe. She walked back to the bed carrying the syringe in a kidney dish, which she placed beside the bed. Shehu had closed his eyes wearily and his respiration was loud and strained.

'Shehu,' Susan said softly. The tired young eyes opened and stared up at the strange white nurse.

Gently, she turned him on to his side, selected the upper and outer quadrant of the thin brown buttocks, and swabbed the skin with antiseptic.

If I'm very careful, he won't feel a thing, she thought as, swiftly and expertly, she directed her syringe towards the required place.

Good, he hasn't moved . . . must have been painless. She straightened up and lifted her small patient back on to his pillows. It's so dry in here. If only the atmosphere were more humid he would breathe easier . . . A steam kettle, that's what I need, she decided.

Susan found her way to the room which served as a treatment room. At the back of one of the cupboards she found what she was looking for. There was even an antiquated paraffin stove to go with it. It took her half an hour to fix up the apparatus, but she was pleased with the result. She had fixed a makeshift tent over the head of the bed and the gentle steam from the kettle was humidifying the atmosphere.

'Is that better, Shehu?' she asked. 'Does that feel any easier?'

'You can hardly expect him to understand English, Nurse,' said a deep masculine voice behind her.

Annoyed, she turned to face the stern blue eyes. 'I realise that, Doctor,' she said coldly. 'But I feel the need to communicate with my patient, and as I don't speak Matalan . . .'

'What a perfectly splendid piece of apparatus,' he interrupted, apparently not listening to her explanation. 'Wherever did you find it?'

'It was in the treatment room,' she answered.

'Must have been brought out to the Dark Continent by Dr Livingstone himself,' he said with a grin.

'I presume so,' she quipped, and as they both laughed their gaze met over the head of the tiny patient. Mike's eyes were full of tenderness as he said,

'You're doing a great job, Nurse.'

'Thank you, Doctor,' she returned calmly, but her pulse quickened as she turned to adjust the kettle. When she looked back again, he had gone.

While Shehu was sleeping, Susan helped with the other patients, giving feeds and drinks and dispensing medicines. The day passed quickly, broken only by a short lunch-break for a bowl of soup in the cookhouse. As evening approached Susan began to feel very tired, but she forced herself to carry on.

Ladi came through from the general section and smiled sympathetically. 'You look exhausted, Nurse Bradshaw,' she said. 'You're not used to our primitive conditions, I think.'

'It's the heat more than anything, Ladi,' Susan replied, with a weak smile.

'The night nurses will take over soon. Then you can rest,' Ladi said encouragingly.

Susan turned to look anxiously at the small patient she had been specialling. 'I should like to explain Shehu's treatment to the night staff,' she said. 'And if his condition worsens I hope they'll call me.'

'Of course, Nurse,' Ladi smiled, impressed by Susan's commitment to her patient.

Some time later, when Susan was sure that the young night nurse knew her job, she went off duty. The black velvet darkness of the tropical night had fallen. The pale light of the moon cast a watery glow over the compound as she made her way towards the cookhouse. Her bones ached for the luxury of a bath, but she felt that it would be straining the water resources too much to ask for one every single day. Perhaps tomorrow . . . ?

Mike was sitting outside the cookhouse, having his pre-dinner cigar. His smile was warm and friendly as their eyes met. 'Not too tired, I hope?' he said gently.

'No . . . I'll survive,' she replied. Her glance took in his clean shirt and casual slacks. He must have changed already. She felt work-stained and grubby as she ran a hand through her rumpled blonde hair. Her cap felt definitely skew-whiff . . .

'You haven't had your bath, yet,' he said, stating the obvious. 'Binta and Fudayin have been waiting for you for ages.'

'Really? How marvellous . . . I hadn't dared to hope . . .'

'But of course—it's essential at the end of a long, hot day. Besides, what's a bucketful of water compared with the comfort of my nursing staff?'

Was he mocking her? Susan couldn't be sure. Hurriedly she left him to puff on his cigar. She had a feeling the blue eyes were following her as she crossed to her hut, but she ignored the disturbing feeling in her haste for the luxurious hip-bath.

The bathing routine was carried out much the same as last night, except that a lamp had been lit and mesh had been placed across the door and window. Susan decided to pamper herself by applying some of the French perfume she had brought with her. Somewhere she remembered reading that perfume attracts insects. Oh well, I don't care . . . Tonight I want to feel like a woman again, not a work machine, she thought.

When she walked back across the compound Mike gave a long, low whistle.

'Not bad,' he said with a grin. Admiration showed in his eyes as they travelled over her full calf-length red skirt and white peasant blouse. 'I'm glad you're wearing mosquito boots under that skirt,' was his cautious comment.

'Of course.' Susan kicked out the toe of a black boot, disturbing the frilly lace of the white petticoat underneath. 'It's my beauty therapy,' she added, feeling pleased with his reaction. 'I find it relaxing to wear something totally feminine.'

'I find it relaxing to look at you, Susan,' he said gently.

'Thank you, kind sir,' she replied, her frivolous tone giving no indication of the urgent beating of her heart.

'Would madam allow me to escort her into dinner?' he asked as he drew himself to his full height.

She took hold of the arm he proffered and they went through the narrow door of the round hut. Tunde smiled his approval at the handsome couple and said something in Matalan. Mike laughed and quietly replied in the same language.

'What did he say?' Susan asked innocently.

'Oh, you wouldn't understand,' Mike said, suddenly serious again.

'I might,' she faltered, but no one enlightened her.

They sat down at the table, at places Tunde had prepared for them. The inevitable yam soup was put in front of them. Susan stifled the temptation to grimace and smiled at Tunde instead. She must be grateful for any sort of food in the midst of this drought area.

Next they had corned beef from one of the tins they had brought. As Tunde was solemnly serving the meat on to Susan's plate, Mike excused himself, saying he was going to fetch something from his hut.

He returned quickly, blue eyes gleaming in the lamplight, as he placed a bottle of red wine and a cork-screw on the table. 'Not a vintage year, but perfectly adequate to go with our succulent menu,' he said with a grin as he deftly withdrew the cork. He poured some into his empty water glass and took a sip.

'Mm, not bad,' he pronounced. 'This will help the digestion, Susan. Drink your water.' She obeyed and then watched as the sensitive hands poured wine into her glass.

He lifted his glass to hers. 'To the most beautiful woman in the room,' he said in a jocular tone, but there was an earnest look in his eyes.

She sipped her wine gently and made no reply.

For dessert there was paw-paw. The soft, orange-coloured tropical fruit was surprisingly succulent, and tasted even more agreeable when washed down with a second glass of wine. Susan's head was beginning to swim. She laughed gaily and covered her glass with her hand when Mike offered her a third refill.

'No thanks, Mike. I'm falling asleep already,' she said. 'I shall need a clear head in the morning.'

He smiled at her and put the bottle down on the table. 'You're enjoying your work here, aren't you, Susan?' he said gently.

'Very much—I only wish there was more we could do,' she replied wistfully.

'I know what you mean. I feel like that every time I come out here.'

The effects of the long day and the wine were making Susan drowsy. Her eyelids drooped for an instant and she gave a start, gathering all her remaining strength to stand up.

'I'm going to bed, Mike,' she said.

'Must you?' His blue eyes sought hers, but she avoided them. 'I thought we could go for a stroll in the moonlight.' His tone of voice was light and teasing, but it sent shivers down her spine. Hurriedly she went towards the door.

'No . . . I must go,' she said with a firmness of resolve she didn't feel.

Outside, under the twinkling stars, she took a deep breath of the hot dry air. He's only feeling lonely, she thought. Probably missing his beautiful girlfriend . . .

She crossed hurriedly to her hut and was soon safely tucked inside her mosquito net. Her sleep was deep and untroubled by dreams of any kind, so it was with alarm that she awoke in the middle of the night to find someone standing by her bed.

By the light of the moon, and through the mosquito net, she could make out the tall figure of a man. As her eyes became accustomed to the dimness she realised that it was Mike. Her heart thumped wildly, and instinctively she pulled the sheet up round her bare shoulders.

'Mike!' she cried.

'I'm sorry to wake you like this.' His voice was tense and anxious. 'The night nurse came to find me—she's worried about Shehu. I need your help—we may have to do a tracheostomy . . .'

Susan's mind shot into action, her professional training overcoming her initial embarrassment at finding him in her room.

'I did knock on your door,' he was saying. 'But you were sleeping so soundly . . .'

'Yes, yes. I'm awake now,' Susan said

hurriedly. 'I'll be with you in just a moment.'

'Thanks,' was the brief reply, as he strode quickly out through the door.

Her white uniform dress was laid out ready for morning. It was only seconds before Susan had it on. As she ran across the compound she fastened the buttons, arriving at the clinic hut adequately dressed. There had been no time to put her cap on—no matter. She ran a hand quickly through her short blonde hair, smoothing it back off her forehead.

Pray heaven we're in time, was her only thought.

She swallowed hard as her eyes focused on the tiny brown figure of her patient as he struggled for breath. His respirations were shallow and rapid and his head was bathed in sweat. Susan felt for his pulse—it was weak and excessively rapid.

Her eyes met Mike's across the bed. 'We must be quick,' he said quietly. 'I've asked the night nurse to prepare the treatment room. Go and check that everything's ready for an emergency tracheostomy. It's our only chance . . .'

Susan hurried across the unit to the doors of the treatment room. The young Matalan nurse turned with a look of relief on her face when she saw Susan. She was scrubbing down the rough wooden table in the middle of the room. An assortment of instruments lay on a trolley by the side of the table. A quick glance showed Susan that the nurse had no idea what would be required.

No time for elaborate theatre technique— every second counts in this life-or-death operation, Susan thought as she swiftly prepared the necessary instruments.

She laid out two tracheostomy tubes—Mike could chose which one he required—two scalpels, one for the skin and one small tenotomy-type knife, for opening the trachea; dissecting forceps, fine curved dissecting scissors . . .

The door opened and Mike carried the small patient in. Susan could see Shehu was in an advanced state of dyspnoea as Mike laid him on the table. Gently she placed a sandbag high under the thin brown shoulders, so that his head was hanging down over the end of the table, supported in the hands of the Matalan nurse.

Mike spoke in gentle, soothing tones to his young patient as he administered a local anaesthetic to the throat. Susan handed Mike a scalpel, and his incision, between the third and fourth rings of the trachea, was swift and skilful. Quickly she leaned across to stem the flow of blood, before handing him the smaller scalpel for opening the trachea.

Seconds later, Mike had inserted the tracheostomy tube and there was a dramatic change in Shehu's breathing. Already the respiration rate had fallen and his discomfort had eased. The young Matalan nurse, wide-eyed with fear, spoke quietly to Mike in her own language.

He smiled gently and said, 'Don't worry, Nurse—it's only a temporary measure, while his throat is swollen. We should be able to remove the tube in a couple of days and he'll breathe normally again—especially when the antibiotics start working.'

Susan was fastening tapes round Shehu's neck to keep the tracheostomy tube securely in position. Gently she raised the small head and held him against her in an upright position. Mercifully, he appeared to have fallen asleep. She looked across the table at Mike.

He swept a hand through his fair hair, which was tumbling down over his forehead, and their eyes met in a long, satisfied look.

'Well done, Nurse Susan,' he said softly.

She smiled back at him. 'Well done, Doctor,' was her quiet reply.

They both looked fondly down at their slumbering patient.

'I'll take him back to his bed,' Susan said quickly.

'Here, let me carry him,' Mike insisted, taking the small bundle from her arms.

Together they put Shehu back into his bed, propped upright against the pillows. Susan checked that there was still water in the steam kettle; it took her a further half-hour to show the young nurse how to keep the tracheostomy airway clear. She prepared a tray with the necessary requirements and placed it by Shehu's bed, checking carefully that she had got everything—gauze swabs, dressings, tracheal dilators.

'Why don't you go and have some rest now, Susan?' Mike had come up quietly behind her.

'I really don't think I should leave Shehu. Our night nurse is very willing but she lacks experience,' she said worriedly.

'That's OK. I'll stay,' Mike assured her.

'But . . .' she started.

'No "buts" about it,' he said firmly. 'Off you go and get your beauty sleep.'

She flashed a grateful smile and bent to wipe the damp forehead of her tiny patient. As she did so her arm brushed across Mike's sleeve. The contact was like an electric current. They both looked at each other for a brief moment before Susan hurried away.

The dark tropical night was giving way to the dawn as she settled back into her bed and fell into a deep, contented sleep.

CHAPTER SEVEN

SUSAN AWOKE feeling refreshed after her deep sleep. The hot rays of the sun were filtering through into the hut, and from outside in the compound she could hear the gentle clucking of the chickens as they pecked at the dry, beaten earth. What was the strange sensation creeping over her as she gathered consciousness? She felt so happy . . . Her head seemed light as a feather . . . Her body was tingling with anticipation of the coming day . . . I'm in love . . .

It came to her in a flash—all the classic signs and symptoms, as if it were a medical case. Well I *am* a medical case to allow myself to fall for that unpredictable, arrogant doctor, she thought. In a couple of days we'll be back in civilisation, and I'll just be one of his many admiring nurses. He'll have no time for me when he gets back to his sophisticated Janice . . .

She pulled herself together and dressed hurriedly, her mind dwelling now on the serious events of the night. I hope Shehu is still improving, she thought. I'll go in and see him before I have breakfast.

She went out of the hut into the bright sunlight, walking quickly across to the clinic and along into the isolation unit. Mike was sitting beside Shehu's bed, a pair of forceps in one hand, a swab in the other, and his eyes closed in sleep. Susan smiled down at the slumbering figure. He seemed to sense her presence because the blue eyes opened; as they focused on her he gave a lingering smile, and her heart turned over.

'I must have fallen asleep,' he said.

'How's Shehu?' Susan asked, quickly turning her attention to the patient and feeling pleased with what she saw. 'My, that's an improvement.' She took hold of the tiny wrist to feel his pulse, and nodded at Mike in approval.

'Yes, he's out of danger now,' Mike agreed. 'I've explained treatment to the nurses, but you'd better special him initially.'

'Have you told him why he can't talk?' she asked, looking down at Shehu's trusting brown eyes.

'Of course,' Mike said. 'Now, what about you? Have you had breakfast?'

'Not yet,' she admitted. 'But . . .'

'Go and have breakfast, and I'll stay till you return,' he said firmly.

Susan looked fondly at the handsome, masculine frame folded uncomfortably in the small cane armchair and smiled. 'OK, but I won't be long. You look all in.'

'I'm all right,' he said.

Obediently she went back through the unit and over to the round hut for coffee and bread.

Several minutes later she was back, ready for action.

Mike's eyes brightened thankfully as she approached, and he stood up. 'I'll take a couple of hours off and get some sleep. Call me if you need me, Susan.'

'Yes, I will,' she said, avoiding his eyes. She gave her full attention to Shehu, and all unsettling thoughts of Mike disappeared with his retreating steps.

Better test Shehu's ability to swallow, she thought, as she poured a little water into a cup. Gently she put her arm round the small boy and eased him forward until his mouth took in some of the fluid. She watched carefully as he swallowed without coughing.

Good . . . no complications there. She gave him another drink and then settled him back on the pillows. Deftly she removed the inner tube from his throat and cleaned it in sodium bicarbonate with the aid of some narrow ribbon gauze and a pair of sinus forceps. No suction apparatus here—the inner tube must be kept clean.

Swiftly she replaced the tube into the outer case of the tracheostomy, watched all the time by those patient brown eyes.

'Good boy,' she murmured, thinking, I don't mind if he doesn't understand my actual words; he must gather something from my tone of voice. She smiled down at him and was rewarded by a weak smile in answer. I wonder where his mother is? Must ask Ladi when she comes through, she decided.

About an hour later, when Ladi called in at the isolation unit, Susan asked her about Shehu's mother. Ladi's warm brown face broke into a broad smile.

'We are very lucky—only this morning I found her. She's in the adult section, suffering from malnutrition. We're feeding her up because she's been too weak even to talk to us before. At last we're getting some response and she's been asking about her son Shehu. From her description, I'm sure he's our little tracheostomy patient.'

'Well, that's good news,' Susan said happily. 'Early days for a reunion, though.'

'Oh, yes. They're both too weak at the moment,' Ladi agreed. 'We'll get them together at the end of week.'

Susan nodded and looked down at her small patient. He was sleeping peacefully, so she took off her specialling gown and went off to help with the baby feeds.

It was another long hot day in the unit, with barely time for a midday break. By nightfall, when she went off duty, Susan was soaked in perspiration and longing for the luxury of her hip-bath. She stepped into it gratefully as soon as Binta and Fudayin left her.

Mm, that's good . . . Susan found herself

tingling with anticipation at the approaching evening. Funny how the thought of simple food in primitive surroundings could make her feel so excited. Her head was analysing the situation, but her heart seemed to be winning . . .

She dressed carefully in the white cotton slacks and blue shirt she had worn on the first evening, not trusting herself to wear the skirt and blouse of the night before. It had caused too much of a stir, and she was trying to remain cool. It would be madness to show her true feelings. As she glanced nervously in the small hand mirror she thought how strange it was to feel like this. Whenever Andrew had taken her out to some expensive restaurant in London, her reaction had been one of total calm. But here she was trembling like a silly schoolgirl . . .

She took a deep breath and went out into the warm velvet of the night.

'Thank you, Binta,' she said to the young girl waiting outside.

Binta smiled. How pretty the white nurse looks tonight, she thought. Her eyes are sparkling like jewels—she must be in love. Not surprising, with that tall, handsome doctor around all the time.

Unaware of Binta's thoughts, Susan walked across to the round hut. The red glow of Mike's cigar told her that he was already there. He stood up as she came near and held out his hand. Uncertainly she placed hers in his and looked up into his eyes. The tender, far-away look he gave her caused further shivers of anticipation deep inside her. She took away her hand and sat down. Together they watched the moon in silence, Mike puffing gently on his cigar.

Soon, Tunde called them into the round hut and placed bowls of soup on the table. 'Carrot soup,' he said proudly, in his lilting Matalan accent.

'Delicious,' pronounced Susan after the first tentative taste, and Tunde smiled his appreciation as he went back to the stove. He was frying something in a large iron pan, and the sizzling noise helped to drown their conversation.

'Pork chops next,' whispered Mike, with a boyish grin.

Susan looked up doubtfully from her soup. 'Where have they come from?' she enquired.

'Don't ask,' said Mike. 'We're being honoured, I think. Someone must have killed a pig.'

'Oh—how nice,' she murmured, and they both burst out laughing. Tunde turned round from the stove, and Mike composed himself enough to say, 'Good soup, Tunde.'

'Yes, sir.' Tunde returned to his cooking.

Susan's doubts were dispelled when the chops were served. Tunde had made a sauce of onions and tomatoes, and the result was most appetising.

'You know, Mike, I feel quite guilty eating like

this when so many of the Kulani tribe haven't got enough food,' Susan said.

'They wouldn't thank you for any of this,' he shrugged. 'When the maize crop fails they go hungry because that's their staple diet. Western ideas on food are incomprehensible—positively distasteful to them.'

'I suppose you're right,' she said thoughtfully.

Mike reached for the bottle of wine they had started the night before. 'Better finish this— it'll go off if we don't,' he said with a smile. 'Tomorrow I'll bring another one.'

Tomorrow, she thought, as the long, sensitive hands poured wine into her glass. There's tomorrow, and the day after, and then back to civilisation, where this wonderful, exhilarating feeling will evaporate like a puff of smoke.

They took their coffee outside and sat under the stars, listening to the night sounds out in the bush. An owl hooted in the distance. 'I didn't know there were owls in Africa,' said Susan.

'Oh yes, but you rarely see them. As in England, they're mainly nocturnal.' He was studying her face, outlined in the moonlight. 'You know, Susan, you remind me . . .'

He broke off, and she turned to look at him.

'Yes?' she asked breathlessly.

'Oh, it's nothing,' he said briefly, his voice changing to a harsher tone. 'I'm tired, so I'll say good night.'

Surprised at his sudden abrupt manner,

she watched as he stood up, grinding his cigar into the dust. 'Good night, Mike,' she said coolly.

Unable to help herself, she stared at the retreating figure as he strode off. Hot tears welled behind her eyes and she put up a hand to brush them angrily away. But the anger was directed against herself.

She slept fitfully that night, tormented by that recurring face—smiling blue eyes looking tenderly into hers.

'No!' she cried aloud, and awoke with a start. It was still dark, and she found herself longing for the morning.

When it came, she found that yesterday's feeling of euphoria had vanished. Good, she told herself. No point in tearing myself to shreds, wishing for the moon.

She breakfasted alone before going into the clinic to take over from the night nurse who had been specialling Shehu. Her young patient gave her a welcoming smile as she bent to take his pulse. His breathing was slow and rhythmical, she noticed, and his temperature back to normal. She gave him a drink of water before starting to clean out his tracheostomy tube.

Mike came in as she was re-inserting the inner tube.

'I'm hoping to perform a decannulation on him this afternoon, Nurse,' he said briskly. 'Would you prepare him for unassisted breathing.'

'Of course. I'll need a suitable cork,' she replied quickly.

'Ladi has one,' he informed her. 'Would you like me to tell Shehu what we're going to do?'

'Oh, yes please—I don't think my Matalan vocabulary is up to it.'

'Very well.' He sat down on the bed and spoke gently to the small boy in his own language. From the gestures of Mike's hands, Susan could tell that he was explaining how she was going to stop up the airway hole with a cork for short periods, until he could breathe without it.

Shehu listened intently and nodded his head gently to show he understood.

He's a good patient, Susan thought as she went off to find Ladi. She found her in the treatment room searching through a box of assorted corks.

'You may have to cut one down to size, Nurse Bradshaw,' she said. 'How about that one?'

'Yes, that's fine.' Susan picked up the cork and a small knife, and went back to Shehu's bedside.

'I'll do that, Nurse,' Mike said in a cold, professional tone.

Obediently she handed over the cork and watched as he shaped it to fit the entrance to the airway. 'That should do it,' he said at last, concentrating on the intricate task. 'Try that, Nurse, while I talk to him.'

Susan took the cork and fitted it over the airway. Mike's soothing voice held Shehu's attention. The little boy barely seemed to notice anything at first, then his eyes showed their consternation and he gasped for breath. Quickly Susan removed the cork and air flowed through the tube again. Shehu smiled bravely.

'Try again in a few minutes, Nurse, and keep trying,' Mike instructed. 'He understands what you're doing.'

Susan repeated the process at intervals throughout the morning, until Shehu could tolerate complete closure of the airway. He grinned happily at his success.

When Mike returned from a morning with the adult patients his eyes shone with pleasure.

'Well done, Shehu,' he said, then turned to look at Susan. 'I'll remove the tube this afternoon and the stoma will close naturally. Have him ready about three.'

'Yes, Doctor.' The formal reply slipped out automatically, but that seemed to be the way things were going to be from now on, she thought ruefully.

Unwilling to leave her little patient at this stage, Susan asked Ladi to bring her something to eat when she went for her own lunch. Ladi returned with some bread and goat's cheese, which Susan ate hurriedly in the treatment room. Promptly at three o'clock, Mike arrived to perform the decannulation. He spoke gently to Shehu to explain the procedure and, with Susan's help, the operation went smoothly and without any complications.

She settled the little boy back on his pillows after Mike had gone. He closed his eyes and went off to sleep, a happy smile on his lips. She looked down at the tiny brown face and thought, at least that's one good result of our coming out here.

When she went off duty, Susan felt a certain foreboding about the evening. There was none of the delicious anticipation of the previous night. When she found that Ladi was to join them in the round cookhouse she felt positively relieved. There was no wine this evening, just a simple meal of soup and tinned meat, with an orange for dessert. It didn't matter; she wasn't hungry. She kept up the pretence of polite conversation and excused herself as soon as possible.

Back in the little sleeping hut, she found herself looking forward to the return to Kyruba and all the simple pleasures usually taken for granted—like reading in bed, she thought with a wry grin, as she turned out the lamp and crawled under the mosquito net.

CHAPTER EIGHT

LADI HURRIED to meet her next morning as she finished breakfast.

'Nurse Bradshaw, would you like to go out to the bush village with Dr Gregson? He's just leaving, and he says if you hurry up . . .'

Susan looked across to the perimeter of the compound, where an impatient figure was revving the engine of the Land-Rover.

'Well, I'm not prepared for the bush,' she began, but Ladi interrupted in a reassuring tone.

'Don't worry. I've packed everything you'll need. I was to have gone myself, but I've got too much to do here—and *don't* worry about Shehu,' she added with a smile. 'We'll look after him. He'll have to do without you when you return to Kyruba tomorrow.'

Susan smiled at the tireless health worker. 'OK, Ladi—I'd love to go. I'd like to be able to say I'd seen something besides the inside of the clinic.'

She ran across towards the waiting Land-Rover. Mike leaned over and opened the door. 'Hop in,' he said unceremoniously, and pressed on the accelerator before the door was barely shut. Remembering her previous experience at the start of a drive, she hurriedly fastened the seat-belt.

As she clicked it into place, he said mischievously, 'How's your head wound, Susan?'

'Fine,' she replied. 'I'd almost forgotten about it.'

'Better not take any chances today.'

'No, better not.' Susan looked out at the bleak, barren desert plateau, rolling endlessly away into the distance. The wheels of the Land-Rover crunched heavily over the baked earth, carving out their own road as they went along.

'I wouldn't like to get marooned out here,' she said with a shiver.

'That would depend who was with you.' He gave her an oblique sideways glance.

Susan remained silent and avoided those searching blue eyes. He needn't think he simply has to turn on the charm and I'll come running, she thought.

The truck swerved to avoid a thin, hungry-looking bush dog as it ran across in front of them. Susan was flung to one side, but the seat-belt restrained her.

'Phew, that was a narrow one,' Mike said, slowing to a halt. He took a hand from the wheel and casually placed it on the back of Susan's seat. 'Are you all right?' he asked anxiously.

'Yes, I'm OK.' Her reply was breathless.

His hand moved across the back of the seat and

touched her hair. He ran his fingers through the short blonde waves. 'Beautiful,' he murmured softly. 'And such a different colour.'

'Different?' she queried, trying to find the inner strength to move away but fascinated by the nearness of that overpowering, masculine body.

'Yes, different,' he said, a far-away look in his eyes. 'I expected you to have dark hair.'

With a swift, tender movement he cupped her head in his hands and brought her face towards his. Gently his mouth sought hers and her lips parted in delicious anticipation. He kissed her slowly, with a lingering tenderness, and she closed her eyes to savour the blissful moment.

His voice brought her back to reality, as he said quietly, 'We'd better be moving, Susan.'

She realised that she had been holding herself motionless—all her resolves had been broken by a single kiss from that sensuous mouth. Confused, she stared in front of her at the dusty plain, trying to quell the thumping of her heart.

Mike drove on unconcerned, as if nothing had happened. They covered several miles before reaching a group of mud huts built at the edge of an area of dried-up scrub land, which constituted the livelihood of the Kulani tribe. The drought had reduced everything to a bare, dusty existence.

As they approached the village Susan could see a hut which was larger than the rest. A constant stream of natives was going in and out of it.

'Look, Mike,' she said. It was the first time she had trusted herself to speak since that disturbing kiss. 'What's happening there?'

'That's the hut where they keep their idols and fetishes—see the carved posts outside?'

Susan nodded.

'Inside you'll find lots of ceremonial objects—pots and dishes for libations. These represent the attributes of the gods and spirits they worship,' he explained.

'What sort of gods?' she asked.

'The Kulani tribe believe in a high god who is the creator and father of all the other gods of earth, sky, thunder, smallpox and water,' Mike said, bringing the Land-Rover to a halt outside the fetish hut.

'It's fascinating. Do you think we could go inside?'

Mike shook his head. 'It's not a good time, Susan. They are praying desperately for rain. We wouldn't be welcome in there.'

Already a small group of villagers had detached themselves from the worshippers to come over to look curiously at the truck. A couple of small, brown, emaciated boys, their bellies swollen with malnutrition, sat down on the front bumper.

Mike smiled at Susan. 'I think we'll stop here,' he said, climbing down to the dusty roadway.

She followed him and found herself immediately surrounded by Kulani natives, reaching out to touch her white dress. One woman, taller than the rest, had actually taken hold of a lock of her hair and was examining it.

'Mike,' Susan said quietly, 'will you ask them to stop touching me?'

He laughed. 'Oh, come now! It's their natural curiosity. They've never seen a blonde before— and a beautiful blonde at that.'

Ignore him, she told herself, as she shook herself free of the annoying fingers and walked forward. Behind her she could hear Mike saying something in an authoritative tone. Whatever it was he said, the natives got the message and the crowd in front of her parted to make way for their white visitors.

The head man of the village came forward to meet them. It was only by his aristocratic bearing that Susan could tell he was the chief, for he wore the same sparse cotton clothing as the other men. He greeted Mike amicably but totally ignored Susan, who found that she was expected to follow behind the two men as they toured the village.

They went in and out of several of the primitive dwellings, where she was surprised and pleased to see a degree of orderliness which she would have thought impossible in such difficult circumstances. Their main problem seemed to be the failure of the crops and the consequent scarcity of food.

They paused as they came out of one family hut and she spoke quietly to Mike. 'It's the old and the very young who are suffering most, but I like the way the villagers all help each other.'

'Yes, there's a kind of community welfare situation—totally unorganised, but it works.' He smiled down at her and lowered his voice. 'There isn't much we can do here. The village witch-doctor resents our interference, and he has more prestige with them than I do. I'm going to leave some medical supplies with the head man and just hope he'll listen to my instructions.'

The head man had turned to watch them, and Mike hastily broke off to say something to him in Kulani. The wizened old brown face broke into a smile, followed by a long, incomprehensible sentence.

'He's inviting us for elevenses,' explained Mike with a grin.

'Well, I'm glad about that,' Susan laughed. 'I'm simply dying of thirst.'

They followed the old man to a round hut set back from the rest of the village. It seemed dark inside, after the glare of the sun. When her eyes became accustomed to the gloom, Susan could see a thin, shrunken old lady sitting on the floor with a string of bead in her hands. She was running them slowly through her fingers and intoning a subdued incantation. A small boy stepped out of the shadows, carrying a pitcher. He poured some cloudy brown liquid into an earthenware mug and offered it to Mike.

Susan watched as he raised the mug to his lips and took a sip.

'What is it?' she asked nervously.

'It's a kind of cocoa,' said Mike. 'You'll find it quite pleasant.'

'I hope so.' Susan smiled at the little boy who was now holding out a mug for her. She drank dutifully and, to her surprise, found she liked the taste.

Refreshments finished, they all went outside again, much to her relief. She felt uneasy in the dark and gloom of the head man's hut. A woman was sitting beside her own hut pounding and grinding manioc tubers to make flour. Susan watched, fascinated, as she rhythmically raised and dropped the long pestle into the mortar, which was a deep cavity scooped out of a tree-trunk.

'That looks like hard work,' she commented to Mike.

'That's only the beginning,' he said. 'When she's finished pounding it, she's got to grind it all between flat stones and then cook it into balls like little dumplings.'

The small brown baby strapped to the woman's back had been lulled to sleep by the rhythmical movement of his mother's body. Susan instinctively moved her hand forward to pat him on the head—he looked so sweet. Just in time, she stopped herself as she remembered

Mike's admonishment on her first day out . . .

She looked up at him and, from the amused smile on his face, she knew he had noticed. As their eyes met she smiled too. Then hastily she looked away in an effort to control her feelings.

When the tour of the village was over, Susan helped Mike unload the supplies they had brought with them. The head man had instructed two of his young men to carry the boxes to the stores hut, and he listened intently to Mike's explanations about the contents. When he was satisfied that the old man had understood, Mike turned to Susan and said, 'We'll say goodbye now. There's nothing more we can do, apart from praying for rain.'

She gave a wry grin and turned her face to the sky. 'I'm working on that cloud up there.'

'A cloud?' he repeated, looking upwards. 'That's the most promising sign I've seen for weeks.'

He turned back to the head man and pointed to the sky. The old man gave a wide toothless smile and nodded his head. Then, in a spontaneous gesture, the gnarled fingers reached forward and clasped Mike's hand. Susan couldn't understand the Kulani words but she knew he was thanking Mike for his help.

As they took their leave the villagers came out of their huts to wave goodbye. Some of the children ran to the edge of the village, and Susan waved to them until they were out of sight. Then she turned to watch Mike as, hands firmly on the wheel, he negotiated the rugged track. Soon it petered out on to the undulating sandy soil of the dry plain.

'There's a small valley, about a mile from here, if I can find it,' Mike said. 'We should be able to get some shelter from the sun there, so we can eat our lunch.'

The Land-Rover bounced over the dry earth towards a narrow ridge. Mike stepped on the brake as he swung the vehicle into the shade of a wizened palm tree.

'Believe it or not, there used to be a deep river here,' he said, as he jumped down to the ground.

Susan looked at the dried-up river bed. 'Let's hope the rains come soon, Mike.' They both looked up at the blue sky and saw that the white cloud was bigger, and had been joined by another, blacker-looking, mass.

He smiled. 'Don't watch it, Susan—it'll go away if we do. I've seen skies like that before, and it was weeks away from any rainfall. Help me unpack the food.'

He lifted the wicker-work food box under the tree, and opened the lid. Susan started to unwrap the various packets inside. 'Isn't Ladi wonderful!' she exclaimed. 'I'd no idea I was coming on a picnic today.'

'And, what's more, I think your table and stools are still in the back somewhere.' Mike rummaged around and found what he was looking for. 'Here they are.' He fixed them firmly on the ground, and Susan spread out the food.

'The beer's warm, I'm afraid.' He handed a can to Susan.

'Doesn't matter; can't have everything. I should say we're doing pretty well,' she said, surveying the table.

There was bread, goat's cheese—rather runny, but still edible—a tin of corned beef, some odd-shaped tomatoes, and a couple of oranges.

'It's not the Ritz but perhaps we can have an end-of-safari celebration dinner tonight. I've still got a decent bottle of wine left, back at Shuna.' Mike's voice sounded casual, but Susan's pulse beat rapidly.

'Sounds great,' she said, hardly recognising her own voice. She bent over the table to spread some cheese on her bread, and Mike busied himself with the tin opener. They both ate hungrily and finished most of the food.

'Mm, that was good.' He leaned back against the tree and watched her thoughtfully.

She could feel that his eyes were upon her, but it was several seconds before she lifted her face to meet his gaze. The liquid tenderness in those blue eyes disarmed her.

It's madness, I know, but I can't help the way I feel, she thought as she fought to control her breathing.

Suddenly he reached towards her, and his strong arms were round her shoulders. He pulled her to her feet and moulded her body against his. Her head swam dizzily, feebly telling her to resist this unattainable man, but her heart won. When his mouth crushed hers she responded uncontrollably to his passion. Her arms went up around his neck, her fingertips smoothing themselves into his fair hair. She could feel the mounting excitement in the strong contours of his manly frame, and for a few moments time stood still . . .

A loud crack of thunder brought her back to earth and Mike's arms released her. At first she thought she must be dreaming, for the heavens opened and torrential rain poured from the skies. A vivid orange flash of lightning illuminated the whole of the dusty plateau.

'Mike, it's raining!' she cried in delight. 'It's raining!' Warm rivulets of water cascaded down her face as she danced for sheer joy on the dampening ground.

'It's raining,' she repeated, over and over again, until he took her in his arms once more and silenced her with a kiss.

'You're going to be soaked,' he said tenderly. 'Let me get you into the truck. We must drive back before the road becomes impassable.'

He swept her into his arms and lifted her effortlessly up into the shelter of the Land-Rover, where she sank blissfully back in her seat. She was vaguely aware of Mike running backwards and forwards, packing the things away, but the unreality of the situation had convinced her she was dreaming. She closed her eyes and gave in to a joyous oblivion, as they ploughed their way through the storm . . .

When she awoke they were approaching Shuna. She yawned and stretched in her seat, looking out at the unaccustomed puddles of the muddy track. The rain was lighter now, and there were breaks in the clouds, showing patches of bright blue sky.

'It looks as if it's going to stop,' Mike said in a disappointed voice. 'I hope that wasn't just a one-off attempt.'

'So do I,' Susan agreed, but she wasn't thinking about the weather. She allowed her eyes to dwell on the handsome sun-tanned face for a few moments before she sat up and reached for her bag.

I must look an absolute sight . . . Where's my comb? Where's my mirror? She hunted through the bag and ran a comb through her hair. The eyes that stared back at her in the mirror were still the same, but she felt so different now, so happy . . .

'My God, what's happened?' Mike's voice broke in on her thoughts. 'Look at that, Susan.'

She looked in the direction he was pointing. On a flat stretch of ground outside the perimeter of the Funa clinic stood a small light aircraft. Its bodywork was white, with distinctive blue markings on the tail and wings.

'That's the aeroplane we charter in Kyruba if we've an emergency at the hospital,' he continued, accelerating through the muddy puddles. 'It's expensive to hire so there must be a real problem down there.'

The Land-Rover hurtled towards the ring of mud huts and screeched to a halt in front of the clinic. Two men and a woman were sitting under the veranda, by the wooden steps. Susan immediately recognised the tall slim woman wearing a cream designer safari suit, enhanced by a red silk Chanel scarf tied casually at the neck. The toss of that long dark hair was unmistakable.

Janice was sitting between Dave and the distinguished-looking man Susan had seen at the MBC concert. She leapt to her feet and rushed down the steps as Mike got out of the Land-Rover.

'Mike, darling,' she called. 'Wherever have you been? I was so worried.'

She clasped his hands in hers and reached up to kiss him. Susan turned away, unable to bear the sight of their embrace. Dave came across and opened the door.

'Hello, it's good to see you,' she said as he helped her down.

'Come along, Mike,' Janice was saying. 'I want you to meet a very dear friend of mine, Guido Vincenzi.' The two men shook hands and Susan waited uncertainly to be introduced.

'Oh, Nurse,' Janice said, as if she had only just

noticed her existence. 'Come and meet Guido—
you must have seen some of his films. He
directed *The Moon and Tomorrow, Live For
Today*, and—oh, lots of others,' she babbled on,
obviously very proud of her famous friend.

The tall, greying Italian film director smiled at
Susan and held out his hand. She was suddenly
aware of her dishevelled appearance when
compared with the immaculate Janice.

'What are you all doing here?' Mike asked in a
puzzled voice.

'Guido's on location in Nigeria. He's got a few
days off from filming, so he came over the border
to see me, and we decided to hire a plane . . .'

'Correction, my dear,' interrupted Guido in a
heavy Italian accent. '*You* decided to hire a
plane . . .'

'Oh, well, it comes to the same thing,' she said
with a simpering laugh. 'OK, *I* decided to hire a
plane and fly out to see you. I'll be able to claim
some of it on expenses because I'm also doing a
programme on the drought. Looks as if I only
just got here in time.' Again the same tinkling
laugh.

'And where do you fit in, Dave?' asked Mike
quietly as Janice paused for breath. 'What I'd
like to know is who's looking after the emergency
unit while we're both away?'

'Richard Brooks offered to stand in,' said
Dave hurriedly. 'It's only for a few hours, and
Janice can be so persuasive . . .'

'It's not his fault, darling,' Janice purred, looking beseechingly up into Mike's eyes. 'I asked him to come so that I can take you back with me.'

Mike stiffened. 'What are you talking about, Janice?' he asked with ominous calm.

'I've got a dinner party tonight, darling. You simply must be there.'

'So you charter a plane just to come out here . . .'

'Oh, don't be cross with me, Mike,' Janice purred in a wheedling voice. 'I've missed you so much. Dave can drive the Land-Rover back tomorrow. Your work here is finished, and you know how much they need you at the hospital.'

Mike smiled his boyish grin. 'You've got it all worked out, Janice, haven't you?' He ran a hand through his fair hair in mock desperation. 'But what about your radio assignment on the drought?'

'Oh, I've seen all I need to see,' she replied with a shudder. 'Awful primitive conditions. Your health worker took me round. I don't know how you and your dear little nurse have endured it.'

'Her name's Susan,' said Dave quietly.

'Oh yes—we saw you at the concert, didn't we, dear?'

Susan turned away. She had the awful feeling that she was going to burst into tears. Her voice sounded muffled when she spoke. 'I must go and change—my clothes are still wet. We were out in the rain . . .'

'Susan!' Mike's imperious voice made her turn to face him. 'I'm going back with Janice.' He sounded as though he had just made a major decision; his eyes were those of a stranger.

'Yes, I know,' she said bleakly. 'Goodbye, Mike.' Somehow she made it back to her hut before the tears began to flow. She stripped off her wet clothes and, wrapping herself in a towel, climbed into the narrow bed.

When she heard the sound of the plane taking off she dried her eyes and pulled on a clean uniform. The romantic interlude was ended. Silly of me to think it could last, she thought, as she buttoned her dress. Her eyes looked red and weepy as she stared into the mirror. She fumbled in her bag for some sunglasses. There, that's better—Dave won't see through that.

She went out into the bright sunlight and crossed to the clinic, where she found Dave doing a round with Ladi. He grinned amiably at her.

'What's with the dark glasses, Susan?'

'Conjunctivitis,' she said lightly.

'Oh, dear—is it bad?' he asked, gently.

'No, I think it's clearing. How are you getting on here? Need any help?'

'Ladi's doing a great job,' replied Dave. 'We're just going to check on your tracheostomy case. That was a stroke of luck having you and Mike here.'

'Yes, wasn't it,' she said as they went through to the isolation unit. Shehu smiled happily when he saw them approaching.

'Hello, Susan,' he said shyly in a soft, lilting accent.

Susan smiled. 'Nothing wrong with your larynx now, Shehu.' She felt for his pulse and was pleased with its regularity. His respiration was normal too. 'Has he seen his mother yet, Ladi?' she asked.

'Yes, I brought her through this morning for a short time,' Ladi replied.

'Good . . . I'm going to miss you, little man,' she whispered.

The smile on the brown face didn't change. He can't understand me, she thought. I'll just go away quietly. There won't be time to see him tomorrow.

'Goodbye, Shehu,' she said gently.

The eyes showed that he understood, for he reached out a small brown hand towards her. She took the little fingers in hers and squeezed. 'You've been such a brave boy.'

She turned and walked out of the unit, and the large brown eyes followed her, unblinking.

As darkness fell, Susan and Ladi took Dave into the little cookhouse for a farewell dinner of carrot soup, tinned meat and paw-paw. It was not the celebration Susan had anticipated earlier in the day. If Mike had been here . . . But he wasn't. She forced her mind back to the present. It had been good while it lasted, but it was over.

CHAPTER NINE

THEY MADE an early start next day. The sun had barely risen when Susan turned to wave to Ladi, Binta and Fudayin. She watched until the mud huts of Funa were out of sight, and then turned her attention to the road ahead. Yesterday's heavy rain had caused havoc with the surface, creating muddy pot-holes into which the tyres sank. Dave had to keep up a good speed so as not to get bogged down.

They took a break at lunch-time, in the same place where Susan and Mike had picnicked on the outward journey. She deliberately avoided thinking about it as she looked out across the now swollen river, which had lapped around the mud-guards of the Land-Rover as they crossed. The past was over—finished. No point dwelling on what might have been . . .

They arrived back at Kyruba in the early evening. It seemed strange to be driving through busy streets—all that traffic! The sun's rays were low on the horizon as they drove along the marina. The cruise ship had gone, but another luxury liner had taken its place amid the myriads of brightly-coloured sailing vessels and fishing boats. Susan felt a pang of excitement as they approached the hospital gates. Only five days since she left, but it seemed like a lifetime. So much had happened . . .

Dave stopped in front of the nurses' home and carried her bags up the stairs.

'How about a drink tonight?' he asked, pausing on the top step.

'Not tonight, Dave. I'm absolutely whacked. Another time . . .' she said.

'Yes, sure.' He watched until she turned the corner of the corridor and then went back down the stairs, shaking his head. Susan had changed—something must have happened while she was away. I wonder if Mike . . . No, he thought, impossible! She's not his type—too warm and sensitive. No, Janice is the girl for Mike—cool, sophisticated . . . He jumped into the truck and drove round to the hospital car park.

Susan opened the door and went into her little room. She closed the door and leaned heavily against it for a second, drinking in the clean, comfortable atmosphere. Yes, it was good to be back. Over on the dressing-table she could see a letter with an American stamp. Andrew!

His letter was full of praise for the American way of life, the super efficiency of the hospital in which he was working, the marvellous social life . . . Not a word to say he was missing her, except a brief passage at the end.

'When you've finished exploring the Dark

Continent, why don't you come over to see me in the civilised world? You'd really enjoy life out here.'

She smiled to herself as she folded the letter and put it away. I might just do that, Andrew . . .

There was another note on her dressing-table. 'Mrs Brooks phoned—says, will you ring her back.'

Mrs Brooks? Who's Mrs Brooks? she wondered. Oh, Kate, of course. Wonder what she wants. Well, it'll have to wait until I've had a shower—oh, the sheer luxury!

As the cooling water cascaded over her hot body, Susan began to feel normal again. The unreality of the past few days faded away and she came back to life. Dressed in cool cotton slacks and a shirt, she went down to the telephone booth in the foyer.

'Kate? It's Susan.'

'Oh, thank goodness you're back,' came the voice at the other end. 'Richard thought you might have problems with driving, after the heavy rain.'

'It wasn't easy, but Dave's a good driver.'

'Dave? I thought you went with Mike.'

'I went with Mike, but came back with Dave,' Susan explained casually. 'Mike flew back with Janice—didn't Richard tell you? He stood in for Dave.'

'No, he didn't,' Kate said. 'It all sounds very

complicated to me. I've hardly seen Richard for days—he's been terribly busy at the hospital.'

'You can blame us,' Susan said.

'I will,' replied Kate, and Susan could hear the laughter in her voice. 'Anyway, what I wanted to ask you was, are you free tomorrow evening?'

'Heavens, Kate, I've no idea. I've only just got back—feel as if I've landed from the moon. Why? What's on?'

'Richard and I are having a party to celebrate our second wedding anniversary.'

'Two years! Is it really that long? You *old* married lady—congratulations!'

'Thanks—well, how about the party then?'

'Kate, I'll move heaven and earth to be free tomorrow evening, otherwise I'll come on later if I can get a lift from someone. Who's coming, by the way?'

'Oh, the usual crowd. John and Helen Miller— you know; he runs the Ikawa Nursing Home, where I used to work—and Julie who nurses there. Then there'll be Mike and Janice . . .'

Kate's voice droned on as she listed the guests, but Susan had stopped listening.

'Susan, are you there?' Kate was saying. 'You've gone very quiet. I can't hear you. Have we got a fault on the line?'

'No, it's OK, Kate, I'm here.' Susan found her voice with difficulty. 'I was thinking there'll be hardly any medical staff on duty.' She gave a dry little laugh.

'Oh, I've left a few,' Kate replied. 'But I'll bet the bleepers start going just as I'm serving supper. I must dash—Jonathan is getting impatient.' Susan could hear Jonathan's cries in the background. 'Goodbye—see you tomorrow.'

Susan put the receiver down and went back to her room. She suddenly felt very tired again— much too tired to go across to the hospital for supper. An early night, that's what she needed, she thought.

As the sun rose out of the sea, Susan leapt out of bed. She was looking forward to getting back to the emergency unit. The hospital dining-room seemed like a four-star restaurant by comparison with the simplicity of Funa. Susan relished the succulent grapefruit, the hot coffee, and, luxury of luxuries—real toast!

Feeling well and truly fortified for the exertions of the day, she went through to the Emergency Unit. Sister Obutu looked up from her desk in Outpatients and gave her a beaming smile.

'Welcome back, Nurse Bradshaw. We've missed you. Did you have a successful expedition?'

'We did what we could, Sister,' Susan replied. 'I wish we could have done more.'

'One always feels like that, after these trips into the bush, Nurse,' said the older woman. 'Still, we must thank God for the beginning of the rains. Things will get easier when the crops start to grow again.'

'I hope so.' Susan was thoughtful. 'What would you like me to do, Sister?'

'We've got a lot of patients waiting to be seen here in Outpatients,' Sister replied. 'So you could work here today.'

'Fine. I'd like that. But do tell me, Sister, how are things going in Children's? How's Mbau?'

'He's doing very well. Burns healing nicely, but I had to splint his arms, now that he's moving about,' Sister said with a grin. 'He just wouldn't keep them still.'

'And Akoy and Wana, our measles cases?'

'Over the worst—no complications, thank goodness—and what's even better, no new measles patients.'

'That's good to hear,' said Susan. 'Well, where shall I start, Sister?'

'We've got a small antenatal group waiting over there. You can do routine checks and refer any problems to the hospital midwifery unit. Dr Gregson will be in shortly.'

'Very good, Sister.' Susan walked quickly across to the waiting refugees, ignoring the palpitations deep inside her.

The patients were huddled together in a group, staring anxiously round them at the unfamiliar surroundings. A young Matalan nurse was with them, trying to allay their fears as they waited to be seen. One weary-looking young woman plucked at Susan's sleeve as she walked past and muttered a long incomprehensible Kulani sentence. Susan paused and looked at the brown, careworn face.

'What is she saying, Nurse?' she asked.

'She says she wants to go back to her children,' replied the young Matalan nurse.

Susan smiled. 'Will you ask her to stay until the doctor has seen her, and find out who's looking after her children.'

The young nurse spoke briefly to the woman, then turned back to Susan to interpret the reply.

'She says her mother is looking after them, but she is very old and tired.'

'Well, tell her we'll be as quick as possible. Antenatal care is very important,' Susan said. 'How many children has she had?'

'Seven,' came the prompt reply. 'But only three have survived.'

Susan sighed, and put her hand on the woman's thin brown arm. She smiled gently into the anxious face and said, 'You must stay until the doctor has seen you.'

The woman seemed to understand, even without the translation. She nodded her head and appeared calmer as she sat down to wait on one of the chairs.

Susan went into the examination cubicles to check that everything was ready. Glancing over the inspection trolley, she was pleased to see that the young nurse knew her job. As she drew back the curtain, smiling her approval, her heart turned over to see Mike standing outside. Although she had prepared herself for their inevitable meeting, she still found that her pulse was racing and the colour rising to her cheeks.

'Is everything in order, Nurse Bradshaw?' The blue eyes were cool and impersonal.

'Yes, Dr Gregson,' she replied, carefully avoiding those penetrating eyes.

'Good—let's get started at once then. I've got a busy schedule today.' His voice was cold and efficient.

Susan beckoned to the woman who had already borne seven children. Better get her back to the surviving brood as soon as possible, although she looks as if she could do with a long rest, she thought.

The woman got up clumsily, her advanced pregnancy making all movements difficult, and ambled forward. Susan took her hand and led her into a cubicle. She pulled the curtains and helped the woman up on to the couch. With difficulty she was persuaded to remove the tattered length of blue and white cloth which was wound round her body. Her arms and legs were like sticks, but the abdomen was round and swollen. Susan covered it with a sheet, which seemed to please her patient.

'We're ready for you, Doctor.'

Mike started by talking quietly to the patient in her own language, noting details of her previous pregnancies. When he had finished, he turned to Susan.

'Apparently this is the first time she has seen a doctor, let alone been inside a hospital. Her mother and various relatives delivered the other babies. Foetal heart beat satisfactory,' he said as he palpated the abdomen.

The woman's eyes had widened apprehensively but Mike spoke a few gentle words in Kulani to reassure her. Next came the internal examination.

'Speculum please, Nurse.'

Susan handed the instrument to Mike, and he began his examination. It revealed that there were no complications.

'Will you take her blood pressure, Nurse,' Mike instructed, going over to the sink to wash his hands.

'Yes, Doctor.' Susan placed the cuff of the sphygmomanometer round the patient's arm and pumped up the rubber bag inside it, watching the level of mercury rise on the glass manometer. Her eyes narrowed as she released the pressure and listened with her stethoscope over the brachial artery, at the bend of the elbow.

'Doctor, I'd like you to check this please,' she said quietly. 'It's too high.'

Mike dried his hands and strode back to the patient to repeat the process. As he removed his stethoscope he nodded in agreement. 'You're right—she'll have to be admitted.'

'But what about her other children?' Susan asked quickly.

'Damn it, Nurse, don't argue!' The blue eyes flashed angrily. 'I'll ask Sister to send someone into the refugee camp to find them, and we'll arrange something with Welfare. The patient is eight months pregnant—her *eighth* pregnancy, high blood pressure . . . What more do you want?'

'I was merely going to say . . .'

'Well, don't,' he snapped. 'Simply admit the patient. You can ask that young Matalan nurse to help me while you're away. At least she can speak the language.'

Tears pricked behind Susan's eyes as she turned away. How could she ever have thought this arrogant man cared for her? Silently she stood by while Mike explained to the woman what was going to happen.

It was a relief to escape from the tense atmosphere to the maternity unit. The patient had closed her eyes in weary resignation as Susan pushed her along in a wheelchair to the bed which the Maternity Sister had indicated.

There was a happy feeling in the ward; the little brown babies slept in cotton cradles at the foot of their mother's beds. A group of young Matalan women were gathered in the middle of the ward, their faces alive with interest as they gossiped.

Just like England, thought Susan, and suddenly felt very homesick. It would be good to get back to London, back to civilisation. As soon as the emergency was over she would return. She would try to forget Kyruba and Funa and . . . she stopped thinking at that point. Only the present mattered—and the future.

When the patient was settled comfortably, Susan returned to Outpatients with some trepidation. For the rest of the morning she carefully avoided any sort of confrontation with Mike, but felt relieved when they had seen the last case.

'I'm going to lunch now, Doctor,' she said quietly. 'If you need me this afternoon . . .'

'No, I don't need you,' he replied in a neutral tone. 'Dr Collins will be working here.'

Susan didn't trust herself to speak. She went out of the cubicle quickly, almost bumping into Sister Obutu.

'Ah, Nurse Bradshaw—about your off-duty today. You can have an evening from five, if you like.' The cheerful brown face smiled into hers.

'Thanks, Sister—that's great; just what I wanted,' Susan said breathlessly. 'That's what I meant to ask you for. I'm going out to Kate and Richard's anniversary party.'

'I thought you might be,' Sister said. 'Who's driving you out there?'

'Er . . . Dr Collins, I think,' Susan responded quickly.

Sister looked puzzled. 'I doubt it, Nurse. He's on duty here all evening.'

'Really? Well there's sure to be someone else,' Susan began.

'Is Dr Gregson still here?' Sister interrupted.

'Do you want me, Sister?' Mike came out of the cubicle, unbuttoning his white coat.

'Yes, Doctor. You and Janice are going to the party tonight, aren't you? Nurse Bradshaw needs a lift and . . .'

'It's perfectly all right, Sister, I can find . . .' Susan began.

'Why, of course we'll give her a lift,' Mike was saying.

Susan avoided looking at him. Outwardly calm, she was inwardly seething with anger. Trust Sister to put her foot in it.

'Well that's settled then,' smiled Sister. 'I do like to know that my nurses are being taken care of. Wouldn't want anything to happen to . . .'

She babbled on and Susan's mind switched off. Somewhere among the chatter she heard Mike's voice.

'Janice has a short programme at seven, so we'll pick you up about eight, outside the nurses' home.'

'Thank you, you're very kind,' was her automatic reply.

She excused herself quickly and sought refuge in the dining-room. Amid the clatter and noise of the hospital lunch she started to breathe more easily.

She found the afternoon's work in Outpatients

easier than the morning's. Dave was not so exacting as Mike, and there were fewer patients. There was time for a coffee-break in the middle of the afternoon, and Susan caught up with all the news. She began to feel less out of touch.

'Only five days away and I seem to have missed so much, Dave.'

'Well, at least you're back in time for the party of the year,' he grinned.

'Mm . . . Pity you'll miss it,' she said.

'No I shan't. I'll come on when I've finished here—about ten, I should say.'

'Oh good.' She brightened visibly. 'Then perhaps you'll bring me home.'

'Delighted, ma'am,' he quipped. 'But how will you get there?'

'Mike and Janice are picking me up,' she replied lightly.

Dave looked across, out of the corner of his eyes. 'That's nice for you,' he said in an innocent voice. They both looked at each other, and burst out laughing.

'You don't like Janice, do you, Susan?' he asked.

'Does it show?'

'Only to an observant person like me,' he said quietly.

'No, I don't like her,' she admitted calmly. 'She's so superficial.'

'You're right, but I think that's why Mike likes to be with her. He hates deep emotion.'

'Does he?' Susan was thoughtful.

'Yes, I don't think he'll ever get married—it would be too big a commitment.'

'And how does Janice feel about all this?' asked Susan, trying to sound unconcerned.

'Oh, she's intent on catching him—can't you see the way she follows him around? She might be successful; you never know.'

'Let's get back to some work, Dave.' Susan put down her coffee-cup, anxious to change the subject.

By five o'clock she had cleared up the Out-patient department. The last case had been seen and she was free to go. Walking across to the nurses' home, her anticipation of the evening was tinged with anxiety.

Once inside her room, Susan searched carefully among the few clothes she had brought out with her, discarding one item after another as unsuitable. No time to go into Kyruba for something new, and anyway they probably didn't have a good selection. How about this white skirt? Susan held it against herself. Maybe . . . Perhaps if I team it with my red blouse?

It was a possibility. She flung the two garments on the bed and went for a shower. What did it matter anyway? She couldn't compete with the elegant Janice, so why bother?

There was plenty of time before she need get ready, so she sat down and wrote to Andrew. It was one of those 'Sorry-I-haven't-written-for-so-long' letters. She described her visit to the Funa clinic, carefully leaving out any mention of Mike. 'The rains have come at last, so the emergency situation will soon improve. I'm not sure what I'll do next . . .'

She lifted her head from the writing desk and stared out of the window at the darkening sky. The scarlet rays of twilight hung over the sea, lighting up the white sails of a tall yacht as it put in to port. She watched as the colours disappeared in the all-consuming darkness of the tropical night.

Time to get ready. It would have to be the white skirt and red blouse. She tried them on and looked at herself in the long mirror. Better than she thought—yes, that would do. And the white strappy sandals on bare brown feet . . . Oh, those awful toe-nails! She reached for her varnish remover and wiped away the tatty remains of the pink polish before repainting them in a colour to match her blouse. She brushed her short hair till it shone—how it's grown! she thought. I'll have to find a hairdresser soon, or cut it myself. She dabbed on some of her French perfume. The fragrance reminded her of the last time she had worn it in Funa.

Promptly at eight, she was standing on the steps of the nurses' home. Mike's sports car was just coming through the hospital gates. As it came to a halt in front of her she braced herself for an encounter with Janice.

'Hello, Susan,' said the brittle voice. 'Can you climb in the back, dear? It's a bit of a squash, but usually there's only the two of us.'

Mike had got out of the car to let Susan in. She brushed quickly past him and settled uncomfortably into the tiny rear space. As she crouched behind them, she felt like an unwanted child being taken on an adult outing. The car shot forward and she slumped lower in the seat.

'When Mike told me we had to pick you up I said, "You're mad—there's only room for two," but he said you were small enough to fit in . . .'

Susan wasn't listening to the prattling voice. She kept her eyes firmly fixed on the stars. The warm night breeze flowing over the open car was a welcome relief from the stifling heat of the day.

Mike and Janice chatted to each other for most of the journey, to the exclusion of Susan, who sat miserably still, longing to arrive at Ogiwa. As the car swung on to the gravel drive, she breathed a sigh of relief.

Several expensive-looking cars were parked in front of the house. The front door was open wide, revealing the bright lights of the interior. There was a sound of soft music, laughter and general chatter. Susan began to feel nervous. It looked like a very grand occasion. Certainly Janice's chic black grosgrain cocktail gown looked eminently more suitable than her own simple outfit.

She uncurled thankfully, and eased herself out

of the back as Mike held open the car door. Her cotton skirt was creased; she paused to smoothe it down and saw that Mike was watching her.

'I hope you haven't been too uncomfortable, Susan,' he said as he looked down at her.

It was the first time he had used her name since they were in Funa together . . .

'No, it wasn't too bad,' she said lightly.

Janice took hold of his arm and propelled him towards the house. Susan was walking quickly in front of them as Kate came out on to the steps.

'Kate!' Susan ran towards her friend.

'Susan; lovely to see you! Let me look at you—you look tired.' Kate eyed her critically.

'No, I'm not,' Susan said defensively.

'Mike and Janice. So glad you could come,' Kate greeted the handsome couple as they came up the steps. 'Long time no see,' she added with a smile.

'Yes, I've been very busy, Kate,' Mike said quietly.

'So I hear.' Kate led them inside. 'Susan tells me you've been out to Funa. Must have been quite an expedition.'

'It was,' he said quickly.

'That's why Susan looks so tired—you've been working her too hard, Mike,' Kate chided as they went into the main sitting-room. 'Now do come and meet the others.'

Susan was introduced to so many new people

she found she couldn't possibly remember all the names. Richard handed her a glass of champagne.

'Drink that, Susan—you look as if you need it,' he said with a wry grin.

'Thanks, Richard.' She sipped her drink, aware that his grey eyes were appraising her with the look of an experienced medical consultant.

'How long since you had a real day off?' he asked.

Startled, she put the glass down on a small table nearby. 'Oh, not long,' she murmured vaguely.

'Too long, I should say. That trip to Funa must have taken it out of you.' His voice showed concern. 'You need a break. Come with us to Tarkawa on Sunday.'

'I don't know if I'm free,' she began.

'I'll speak to Sister Obutu,' Richard said firmly. 'You're coming with us, and that's an order.'

'Yes, Doctor.' Susan's smile of pleasure lit up her face.

'That's better. The treatment's working already. Now, if you'll excuse me . . .' He waved the champagne bottle and moved on to the next guest.

There was a buffet supper, served in the long cool dining-room overlooking the lake. Susan could just see the moonlight reflected on the water. She took a plate and helped herself to some chicken, quiche lorraine and salad.

'Kate, this buffet is marvellous—did you make it all yourself?' she asked, as her friend passed by.

'I made the quiche, but Muhammadu did the rest. Oh, I don't believe you've met John Miller and his wife. They've just arrived. Helen!' Kate called to a pretty young woman with long fair hair and an attractive smile.

She waved from the doorway and came over, followed by her husband, a tall, distinguished-looking man of about forty.

'I want you to meet a very dear friend of mine. This is Susan Bradshaw—John and Helen Miller,' Kate said, eyes shining happily.

Susan smiled. 'I believe you're in charge of the Ikawa Nursing Home, Dr Miller.'

'Yes, that's right. Do you know it?' he asked.

'I came out for a swim with Dave Collins, but you were both in Kyruba that afternoon.'

'Then you must come again soon when we're at home,' smiled Helen.

'Thank you, I'd love to.'

'Ladies and gentlemen.' Richard was tapping a knife against his glass as he tried to attract everyone's attention. 'I want to propose a toast.' The room fell silent; he raised his glass, and his eyes met Kate's.

'To my wife,' he said gently.

'To Kate, to Kate . . .'

The room echoed with the toast, and Kate

looked dangerously near to tears. When everyone was quiet again, Kate cleared her throat nervously before saying, 'For the happiest two years of my life—to Richard.'

Glasses were raised again. More champagne was poured. Susan looked round the crowded room. There was no sign of Mike and Janice— ah, there they were on the veranda, standing still in the moonlight. It looked so romantic. She turned away.

When she next looked, they were coming back inside, hand in hand. Mike raised his glass to Kate and Richard.

'Congratulations you two. Quite an achievement—two whole years of married bliss,' he said, a handsome smile playing on his sensuous lips.

'I can recommend it, Mike,' said Richard. 'When are you going to take the plunge?'

'Perhaps sooner than you think, old man,' said Mike with an enigmatic smile.

Susan looked across the room and saw Janice squeeze Mike's arm. She stood up and went out into the fresh air. Dave had just arrived and was getting out of his car. He waved and came along the verandah.

'Am I glad to see you,' she exclaimed.

'Really? That's nice,' he said. 'Good party?'

'Splendid,' she said convincingly, leading the way back into the house.

A space had been cleared in the large sitting-room and the guests were drifting through to join the dancing. A small group of African musicians were playing on a raised dais.

'Let's dance, Susan,' Dave said.

'Aren't you hungry?' she asked.

'No, I had supper at the hospital,' he replied as he led her on to the floor.

The dancing went on into the small hours. Susan felt herself dropping on her feet. When Dave said he would have to go back, she felt relieved. Mike and Janice had disappeared by themselves about midnight—probably gone on somewhere . . .

She and Dave said goodnight to Kate and Richard. 'Now don't forget Sunday,' said Richard. Then, turning to Kate, he explained, 'Susan's coming with us to Tarkawa.'

'Oh, splendid,' Kate said.

'We'll pick you up at nine o'clock,' Richard added.

'Bring a bikini and a towel,' called Kate, as Susan climbed into Dave's car.

She smiled and waved. 'OK, I'll be there, Kate. Bye.'

Dave let in the clutch and they drove off down the drive and out on to the Kyruba road. There was no traffic in the deserted streets of the town. Soon they were speeding along the marina and in through the hospital gates.

Susan leapt out of the car as they screeched to a halt.

'Thanks, Dave. Good night,' she said briefly.

'Good night, Susan,' he said in a resigned voice.

CHAPTER TEN

THE SUN BEAT down from the clear blue sky as Richard drove along the marina. Kate sat in the back, holding Jonathan on her lap, and Susan was sitting in the front seat. Susan and Kate chatted non-stop from the moment Susan climbed into the car.

'Hey, you two, if I could just get a word in edgeways,' began Richard, with a tolerant grin.

'Of course, darling,' said Kate, smiling. 'I wondered why you were so quiet.'

'Quiet! It's impossible to make myself heard when you two get together. I just wanted to ask Susan if she'd remembered her bikini.'

'Yes, it's in my bag—haven't brought any food, though. I meant to ask the hospital kitchen . . .'

'Oh, that's OK. We've got an enormous picnic. I've brought enough for the five of us—and Jonathan of course.'

'Five?' asked Susan.

'Oh, didn't I tell you? Mike and Janice are coming with us . . . there they are.' Kate waved a hand as they approached the harbour.

Mike's unmistakable sleek-looking sports car

was parked by the water, and Janice was perched on the bonnet in a languid model-girl pose.

'Thank heavens you've arrived,' she said, by way of a greeting. 'I'm scorching in this heat.'

'It'll be cooler on the water,' Kate placated. 'Susan, will you take Jonathan, and I'll help Richard and Mike with the gear. It's the brown and white launch over there.'

'Follow me, Susan,' said Janice, picking her way delicately along the harbour in her precariously high heels.

Susan straddled Jonathan on her hip, African-style, and swung her beach bag over the other shoulder.

'Come along,' called Janice impatiently. Susan gritted her teeth. At least she's remembered my name today . . .

They were soon speeding over the blue water outside the harbour. Kate had fixed a life-jacket on Jonathan. As he crawled excitedly around the boat, she kept her hand firmly clamped to the back of it. Richard steered skilfully through the water, running along the coastline. After about half an hour they reached Tarkawa Bay. He ran the boat close to the shore and Mike jumped out to tie her up.

'What a fabulous beach, Kate,' Susan said, as they walked barefoot through the soft white sand.

'Yes, isn't it? It's like a desert island. You can't get here except by water.'

They had reached a long low hut, built of dried grass and wooden poles. It felt deliciously cool inside, after the heat of the sun.

'This belongs to the hospital staff,' explained Kate. 'Someone built it a few years ago, and we all help to keep it in good condition. It's marvellous for picnics—there's everything you need, except the food, which we bring with us.'

Richard and Mike were stacking the picnic boxes inside the beach house. Jonathan sat on one of the boxes and started to open it with his tiny, exploring fingers.

'No, Jonathan,' Richard said firmly as he lifted his small son off the box. 'Would you girls like to take this inquisitive young man into the sea, while Mike and I check that the barbecue equipment is still in order?'

'Sure; come along, Jonathan,' Susan smiled, reaching over to take him from Richard.

'I think you'd better change first,' he said. 'I'll hold him till you're both ready. Where's Janice, by the way?'

'I think she's still on the beach,' Mike said.

Susan looked through the doorway and, sure enough, there was Janice sitting on a large multi-coloured towel, smoothing sun oil over her deeply tanned skin. She had removed her exotic caftan to reveal a miniscule matching bikini.

'We can change through here, Susan,' said Kate, leading the way through a doorway draped with long strings of African beads.

The beads tinkled as Susan went through into the tiny back room. She stripped off her white cotton slacks and shirt and put on her white bikini.

'That's nice,' Kate said admiringly. 'But you need to get out in the sun more often—get yourself a real tan. Like Janice,' she added with a smile.

'Yes, I'll have to work on it,' Susan said lightly. 'Haven't had much time to lie in the sun, so far. Besides, I thought sunbathing was dangerous out here in the tropics.'

'Not if you take it slowly and use a good sun-tan oil,' said Kate, as she pulled on an emerald green bikini which showed off her seasoned tan to perfection. 'You'll have to come out to Tarkawa with Richard and me more often. There's always a slight breeze by the sea—makes a change from the stifling heat inland.'

'That would be nice—but I don't expect I'll be staying much longer. Things are beginning to ease off in the Emergency Annexe, so I don't think I'll be needed much longer . . .'

'But, Susan, there's sure to be a vacancy in the main hospital. Richard will . . .'

'That's OK, Kate,' Susan interrupted quickly. 'I'd like to move on soon.'

'But don't you like it out here?'

'I . . . I'm getting used to it,' Susan said carefully.

'I know what it is—it's your gorgeous boy-friend in the States,' laughed Kate. 'I knew you were pining for Andrew.'

'Oh, come off it, Kate.' Susan's laughter was forced. 'You don't know anything at all about him.'

'I know he's handsome, fun to be with—you told me that yourself, don't forget. He has written to you?'

'Well, of course he has . . .'

'There you are then, what did I tell you . . .'

'Are you two going to stay in there gossiping all day?' Richard called, in a bantering tone. 'We can hear every word you're saying, so for God's sake don't start talking about us.'

Kate giggled. 'Come on, Susan, we'd better go.'

Jonathan was sitting on the floor, happily clinking the picnic cutlery together and smiling gleefully at the sounds he was making. He lifted up his small arms towards Kate as she and Susan came through the beaded doorway.

'Mama, mama,' he cried.

Kate scooped him up in her arms. 'We'll leave you boys in peace. Come and join us when you've finished.'

They went out into the bright sunlight and ran down the beach to the sea. The elegant figure on the expensive towel remained motionless, her closed eyes turned towards the sun as though performing an act of worship.

Jonathan splashed about in the shallows under the watchful eye of his mother, while Susan swam out from the shore. The waves coming towards her were full and bounding. Susan made a few attempts to swim among them before returning to Kate.

'The waves are too strong for me,' she panted as she strode through the shallow water on to the beach, pushing her soaking blonde hair out of her eyes.

'You'll have to go further out,' Kate explained. 'When you get through the breakers it's as calm as a millpond. Wait till the men come. They'll take you out there.'

'Do you want to have a swim? I'll watch Jonathan,' Susan said.

'No, I'm quite happy splashing around here. Ah, here come the men. Richard! Take Susan out through the breakers.

'Why don't we all go?' Richard said as he and Mike strode down the beach towards them.

'But what about Jonathan?' asked Kate.

'Janice isn't swimming,' Richard said, looking across at her prostrate body. 'She won't mind keeping an eye on him.'

At the sound of her name, the slim figure came to life and gently eased itself into a sitting posture, one well-manicured hand clasped around a slender knee.

'I'm not very good with babies,' she said with a sweet smile. 'They don't seem to like me.'

'Nonsense,' Richard retorted. 'Jonathan likes everybody—he's very easy to get on with, Janice. Or would you prefer a swim yourself?'

Janice shuddered. 'No thanks. I've just put some more oil on, and besides, I don't want to get this bikini wet.'

'That's settled then,' Richard said briskly, with something of the authoritative tone he was used to using in his capacity as senior medical consultant. 'Do you mind coming a little closer to the sea, Janice? I don't think you're near enough to watch Jonathan up there.'

She pulled a wry face and slowly started putting her bottles and lotions into her bag. When she finally moved down the beach, carrying all her gear, the swimmers raced into the sea.

Several yards from the shore, a huge wave bore down on Susan. She shrieked in anticipation of the strong force. 'Kate . . . I'll never get through that one!'

Richard was swimming near. 'Yes, you will,' he called. 'Head down, Susan, and arms forward. There you go.'

In a confusion of thundering water, she forced a way through and, seconds later, emerged triumphant in the calm water beyond the breakers.

'Oh, that was so exhilarating,' she grasped, blinking her eyes in wonder as she looked around at the lagoon-like surface of the sea. 'I'd no idea it would be like this.'

'That's just how I felt, the first time Richard brought me out here,' Kate said, looking shyly at her husband. 'Do you remember, darling?'

'I remember,' Richard said gently, as his eyes met Kate's above the clear blue water.

'When you two love-birds have finished your billing and cooing, we could perhaps do some swimming,' said Mike with a grin, treading water beside the happy couple. The sun was lighting up his fair hair, and Susan was trying not to think how handsome he looked in his sleek black swimming trunks . . .

There was a cry of alarm from the beach.

'Mike! Mike!' They all turned to look. Janice was waving her towel in agitation. 'Come back, Mike. I think . . .' The rest of the cry was drowned by the sound of the waves crashing on the shore.

'I'd better see what Janice wants,' Mike said, as he turned to plunge back through the waves.

'I hope Jonathan's all right,' said Kate anxiously.

'Of course, he's all right,' Richard snorted. 'Janice is perfectly capable of looking after him—and Mike will give us a shout if anything's wrong. Oh, look over there! Can you see the porpoises?'

Susan's eyes followed the line of Richard's arm to where several huge silver creatures, their skin glinting in the sunlight, were leaping in and out of the water.

'Beautiful,' she murmured.

'They're usually here when we come,' Kate said as she swam alongside. 'They seem to like human company. I think they're having a look to see if we're friendly.'

'Don't go too close, Kate,' called Richard. 'You'll scare them away. They're very timid creatures.'

Susan and Kate trod water, held up by the buoyancy of the salty sea, as they admired the superb display. 'I think they're showing off,' Kate laughed. 'It's a special performance for Susan.'

'I think you're right,' agreed Richard. 'Look at that enormous one. Isn't he magnificent . . .'

As if the spectator applause was too much for them, the fabulous shoal suddenly turned and swam away towards the horizon.

'I wouldn't have missed that for anything,' breathed Susan. 'It was certainly worth coming out for.'

'Stay long enough and we'll show you all the delights of the tropics,' Kate said. 'You mustn't think of leaving Africa yet.'

'You're not seriously thinking of leaving, are you, Susan?' Richard's grey eyes were watching her thoughtfully.

'I might,' she answered lightly, striking out into the calm blue water. 'When I feel I'm not needed any more I'll go . . .'

'We'll miss you,' Kate called after the retreating figure of her friend.

Susan swam on with strong strokes until, turning round, she realised she had strayed a long way from the shore. As she hurriedly changed direction she noticed Richard's dark head a few feet away.

He smiled at her. 'Kate thought I should keep an eye on you.'

'I'm glad she did,' said Susan breathlessly. 'I've come further than I wanted to. You should have called me back.'

'I was going to,' he said, swimming beside her. 'But you looked as if you wanted to be alone. I decided you were trying to think things out . . .'

Susan smiled mysteriously. 'Maybe I was.' She changed from a slow breast-stroke to a quick crawl.

As they reached the breakers Richard shouted, 'Go along with this next wave—it should take you into shore. Ready? Now!'

She flung herself on to the crest of the wave and felt herself carried along by its momentous surge. She had no time to feel frightened as she found herself speeding towards the shallow water. It was over in a few seconds and she laughed as she found herself on the shore.

Kate was running down the beach to meet her. 'Well done—you looked like a human surf-board!'

'Kate, that was wonderful!'

'You had me worried when you swam so far out.'

'You needn't have worried, darling,' Richard said. 'She's a strong swimmer.'

Susan looked around for Jonathan. He was still playing happily in the shallow water, a few feet away.

'What was all the panic about, Kate?' she asked.

'Oh, nothing much,' Kate answered quickly. 'Janice thought Jonathan might have swallowed some sand. It won't harm him, even if he has—it'll pass straight through,' she added with a laugh.

Susan looked across the beach to where Janice and Mike were lying side by side in the sun. 'I don't think Janice likes baby-minding,' whispered Kate, mischievously.

'I'm sure you're right,' Susan agreed.

'Time to light the barbecue. Mike, will you give me a hand,' Richard called.

'Sure.' Mike uncurled his long, athletic limbs, and pulled himself to his full height.

'Don't be long, darling,' came the wheedling voice.

Susan watched as Mike smiled down at Janice. 'Is there anything I can do to help, Richard?' she asked.

'Yes, you can help Kate with the salad, in the beach house,' Richard said. 'I suppose Mike and I had better keep an eye on Jonathan. He'll be impossible if we take him out of the water before the food is ready.' He glanced across at Janice, to see if she was going to offer her assistance, but her eyes remained tightly closed.

Susan and Kate ran up the hot sand of the beach and went into the relative cool of the beach house.

'No point in changing,' Kate said. 'We'll be dry in a few minutes in this heat. Can you wash the lettuce, Susan—there's a bowl and some water over there.'

Susan pulled off the outer leaves of the lettuce and poured water into the bowl. Methodically she started to wash each leaf, her thoughts miles away. Kate's voice broke in on them.

'You know, I can't think why you don't get on with Mike. He seems perfectly amenable to me. I don't think he's changed a bit since I first knew him.'

'He certainly seems happy enough today,' Susan said lightly.

'I think he's in love,' Kate said softly.

'You're such a romantic, Kate.' Susan forced a smile on her face. 'But you're probably right.'

'I *know* I'm right. He's got all the signs and symptoms of *l'amour* . . .'

'Oh, don't start that again,' Susan protested hurriedly. 'You make it sound like a disease.'

'What sounds like a disease?' asked Mike, striding in through the doorway.

Susan felt the colour rising to her cheeks. Kate laughed. 'You shouldn't eavesdrop, Mike. You might hear something you shouldn't. Anyway, you're supposed to be helping Richard. It's girls only in here.'

'I came in to look for the matches. Richard thought he'd left them in here . . . There they are.' A strong sun-tanned arm reached across the table in front of Susan, but she kept her eyes firmly fixed on the bowl in front of her. 'Mm, that looks good,' Mike murmured, reaching towards the jar of potato salad Kate was unwrapping.

'Hands off.' Kate playfully tapped his fingers.

He grinned mischievously. 'I can tell when I'm not wanted,' he said, as he beat a hasty retreat.

'See what I mean?' Kate asked when he had gone. 'I find him very easy-going.'

Susan was silent. No point in arguing with Kate . . . 'Where shall I put this lettuce?' she asked after a short pause.

'There's a wooden salad server here. Now, let's prepare the chickens. Smells as if Richard's got the fire going.'

When Susan carried the tray of small chickens out, the blazing fire had been dampened down to a hot, charcoal glow.

Richard took the tray from her. 'We'll put these on the iron bars like this . . .' A delicious aroma of roast chicken was soon wafting across the beach.

'Is that lunch I can smell?' asked Janice, coming to life again. 'Mike, where are you?' she looked around her.

'Over here, my love,' Mike said, as he basted one of the chickens.

'Help me carry my things over, darling,' she called plaintively.

Mike put the basting spoon down and sprinted across the sand. Susan turned away and went back into the hut to help Kate. They carried out the salad, plates, and cutlery and placed them on a rustic trestle table by the fire.

'Thank you, girls,' said Richard, as he lifted a perspiring face above the barbecue. 'Phew, it's hot work! Can you organise the drinks, Mike? I brought some white wine in the cold box.'

'Is it dry?' asked Janice, as she curled herself into a basket-work chair by the table. 'I hate sweet wine.'

'It's medium,' Richard said evenly. 'It's a German hock.'

'Would you prefer water, Janice?' Susan asked sweetly.

'No thank you . . . I shall be quite happy with a glass of hock,' was the injured reply.

Susan could see Kate running into the beach hut, her shoulders shaking. She followed her friends and found her convulsed with the giggles.

'Honestly, Susan, you shouldn't wind Janice up like that,' Kate said. 'She's got absolutely no sense of humour.'

'I know—that's why she annoys me so much,' Susan said vehemently.

'I know what you mean.' Kate grinned. 'And

she's got Mike wrapped round her little finger, hasn't she?'

'Mm . . . Anything else to go out there?'

'No, that's the lot—let's join the others.'

Mike was pouring out the wine when they got back. 'A toast,' he called, handing glasses to Kate and Susan. 'To the happiest married couple in the world—Richard and Kate.'

'Richard and Kate!'

Glasses were clinked. Kate picked up Jonathan and poured some orange juice into his mug. He gulped it down thirstily and clamoured for more.

'I think these chickens are OK now,' said Richard, wiping a hand across his forehead. 'Somebody pass me that big serving dish. Thanks, Susan—there we go.'

Susan held the dish in front of Richard until all the chickens were arranged on it.

'Will you carve, Mike?' Richard asked. 'I'm too sticky for anything. I'll just go and clean up in the beach house.'

'Sure,' said Mike, standing up at the end of the table. 'Scalpel, Nurse,' he called imperiously, and Kate laughed as she passed over the large carving knife. When Richard returned from the beach house, everyone had been served, and the 'oohs' and 'ahs' proclaimed that the chicken was cooked to perfection.

'My compliments to the chef,' said Kate, raising her glass towards Richard.

'You could always get a job in a hotel if they run out of patients in Kyruba,' Mike said with a grin.

'Have some more salad.' Kate was passing the dishes around while Susan coped with feeding the hungry Jonathan. He sat on her lap, spooning in mouthfuls of diced chicken and potato salad, spilling half of it on to her.

'In your mouth please, Jonathan,' she said firmly as she guided his spoon.

'Here—give him to me. You haven't eaten anything yet Susan.' Richard took his son.

Kate produced a huge bowl of fruit salad to finish off the meal.

'Everything always tastes so much better in the open air, doesn't it,' said Kate. 'I'm going to clear away now, because I want Jonathan to sleep in the beach house this afternoon. He gets very crotchety if he misses his rest.'

'I'll help.' Susan jumped up from the table.

They cleared the plates into the beach house and washed them in the bowl. Richard came in carrying Jonathan. The little boy's eyelids were beginning to droop.

'One tired little man,' he murmured gently.

'I'll put him down on the couch,' Kate said.

'Shall I stay with him?' Richard asked.

'No, that's all right. I'll stay. You go out and enjoy yourself,' Kate said, taking Jonathan from Richard.

'I thought we might go for a walk round the

cove,' Richard proposed.

'Yes, that would be lovely—Susan would like the view from the rocks,' Kate agreed as she eased her son gently down on to a cool cotton sheet. 'I'd better not leave Jonathan.'

'OK. See you later.' Richard dropped a kiss on to Kate's cheek.

Susan followed him out of the hut. Mike and Janice were standing close together by the dying embers of the barbecue. Janice was looking wistfully into Mike's eyes.

'Hey, you two,' Richard called. 'Are you coming round the cove with us?'

Janice pulled a face. 'Is it far?' she asked in a delicate voice.

'No, it's not,' replied Richard patiently. 'And the exercise will do you good. Come along now.'

'You sound like an exasperated schoolmaster,' Susan said quietly as they moved away.

'Do I?' he grinned, falling into step beside her.

Mike and Janice followed on at a slower pace. Susan could hear their murmuring voices behind her. They walked along the beach and turned into a rocky cove.

'It's beautiful!' Susan stood still to admire the view spread out before them.

A wide sweep of white sand, interspersed with huge granite rocks, ran down to the clear blue water. Tall palm trees fringed the outer edge of the cove, leading on to thick green hibiscus bushes and wild frangipani.

'It's one of my favourite spots,' said Richard. 'Full of memories.' They walked along the sand and sat down on one of the rocks.

'It's so peaceful,' Susan added. 'Only the sound of the waves . . .' Even as she spoke, a harsh mechanical whirring noise out on the water crashed through the silence.

'Sounds like a speedboat.' Richard stood up and shielded his eyes from the sun. 'Yes; look, Susan—out there.'

He was pointing to a shiny silver boat skimming rapidly towards the beach house bay.

'I wonder who that can be?'

'Guido!' called Janice excitedly. 'It's Guido— oh, thank God for that . . . He said he would come, but I'd almost given up hope. Come on, Mike.'

Susan recognised the distinctive flamboyant figure of the Italian film director as the boat sped nearer to the bay. It went out of sight round the corner of the cove, and she heard the engines cut out. Janice was already running to meet her friend, followed closely by Mike.

Richard sat down again on the rock beside Susan. 'I didn't know he was coming,' he said with a wry grin. 'Not really his kind of place—too quiet.'

'I think it's too quiet for Janice,' smiled Susan. As if in confirmation they heard Janice's voice from the edge of the cove.

'We're going back with Guido, Richard. Goodbye.'

They caught a fleeting glimpse of her as she hurried off again.

'Can't wait to get away,' Richard observed drily.

'I know the feeling,' muttered Susan.

Richard gave her a sharp look. 'What do you mean, Susan?'

'Oh, nothing,' she said lightly, wishing she hadn't spoken.

CHAPTER ELEVEN

THE SOUND of the speedboat engine distracted them for a few moments and then, as the mechanical noise disappeared over the water, Susan sighed. 'They've gone,' she said simply.

'Yes . . . poor Mike,' sighed Richard.

'Why do you say poor Mike?' she asked.

'Isn't it obvious, Susan? He doesn't care for Janice. She's just someone to be with—a beautiful butterfly creature to while away the time with, until he feels strong enough for a real relationship.'

'I don't understand . . .' Susan began, breaking off in mid-sentence as a tall shadow fell across the rock. 'Mike!' she gasped. 'We thought you'd gone away with Janice.'

'Obviously,' said Mike drily, looking down at them. 'Otherwise you wouldn't have been discussing me so openly.'

'Mike, I'm sorry,' began Richard . . .

'That's OK,' he said quietly. His blue eyes were searching Susan's face enquiringly. 'You merely anticipated what I came to say. I've sent Janice away with Guido.'

Susan raised her head in surprise, but saw that Mike's eyes were full of tenderness.

Richard gave a nervous cough and stood up. 'I think I'll go and see if Kate needs me,' he said, but neither of them noticed as he sprinted away across the sand. They only had eyes for each other.

'Mike, I wish you'd explain . . .'

'It's very simple, really,' he said tenderly, kneeling down in the soft sand, beside her. 'Kate never realised I was in love with her. When she married Richard, I thought my heart was broken.'

Susan gave a hoarse laugh. 'That's a very unscientific statement, coming from the eminent Dr Gregson.'

Mike's face was serious. 'Emotions can be unscientific, Susan,' he said. 'For a long time I found it impossible to commit myself, emotionally, until . . .'

He paused and looked carefully at her.

'Until what?' she asked, wide-eyed.

'Until you came, Susan,' he said gently.

'No, I don't believe . . .' she began, but his mouth closed on hers firmly, sensually, driving her into a frenzy of wild desire. Her lips parted and her body melted against his as she surrendered all claims on reality. Yes, this was the end of the dream—this was the fulfilment . . .

She stirred in Mike's arms; they were lying on the soft warm sand. Gently he eased her against him and pulled himself to a sitting position, his back leaning on the granite rock, looking out towards the clear blue sea.

For a few moments neither of them spoke, and then he whispered, 'You know, Susan, since I've met you, I've realised that my heart wasn't really broken; bruised perhaps—but not broken. Kate was right—we were just good friends. You came along and I experienced true love for the first time in my life. I'd been carrying a torch for Kate for so long . . . Would you believe I actually went out with Janice because I thought she looked like Kate?'

'Yes, I'd believe it,' Susan replied softly.

'At first I couldn't understand my feelings for you,' he continued, his hand fondly stroking the skin of her arm. 'I'd never felt like that before. I think I've loved you from that very first moment when I saw you standing out in the sun, feeding the refugees.'

'But, Mike . . . you were so beastly to me!' she exploded.

'I was fighting against my feelings, Susan . . . I didn't want to fall in love—I didn't want to risk being hurt again. But this morning, when I heard you talking of going away . . . perhaps to someone else . . . Susan, *is* there someone else? What about this Andrew?'

'He means nothing to me, Mike,' she said, smiling up into his eyes. 'To quote the old cliché again—we were just good friends. I'd never been in love until I met you . . .'

Once again he silenced her voice with his

urgent, passionate lips, his arms folding her in a sensual embrace. As he gently released her she murmured, 'Mike—what did Tunde say, that night in Funa?'

He smiled mischievously. 'Roughly translated, he said we were a handsome couple—ideally suited to each other—and I agreed.'

'You might have told me,' she said.

'I didn't think you would appreciate it at the time,' he countered. 'Anyway, I've told you now, so if you think Tunde was right you'll have to agree to stay here.'

She smiled happily and wiggled her toes blissfully in the sand. Mike took her face in his hands and gazed into her eyes.

'Susan—will you marry me?'

'Yes,' she whispered, and as the waves pounded on the tropical shore she surrendered herself to his all-consuming embrace.

The sound of engines starting up in the next bay brought them back to reality.

'I think Richard's trying to tell us something,' she laughed, jumping to her feet and brushing away the sand.

Mike reached out a hand to pull her down again. 'Let's stay here for ever, just the two of us,' he murmured.

She playfully avoided his grasp. 'I expect we'll return here often,' she said, feeling suddenly shy about being engaged to the man of her dreams.

Mike stood up reluctantly and took her in his

arms once more, gazing down at her with tender blue eyes. 'We'll bring our children,' he began.

'Hey you two . . . we're just leaving,' Richard called, as he rounded the corner of the cove. He stopped and gave a knowing smile when he saw Susan and Mike locked together.

They broke apart. Then, linking hands, they ran across the warm sand. As they reached Richard he stretched out and shook Mike's hand. 'Congratulations.'

'But I haven't told you anything yet,' countered Mike, his handsome face smiling broadly.

'Nothing to tell,' was Richard's reply. 'I've always hoped this would happen. Let's go and tell Kate. She'll be thrilled.'

For once in her life, Kate was speechless with happiness. But after the initial silence, she couldn't stop talking about the forthcoming wedding. The journey back over the water took on a dream-like quality for Susan. The soft ripple of the waves, the last rays of the sun falling on the sea, and the intense excitement in the boat, as Kate chattered happily on.

Mike and she had to decline an invitation to dinner at Ogiwa House, as Mike had to get back to hospital. 'I've promised Sister I'll look in on a couple of patients this evening,' he told Susan as they walked along the hospital corridor. 'It won't take long, and then we can be alone again for a quiet celebration.'

He paused by the ward door and looked down at her with indescribable tenderness. 'Come in with me, Susan. I can't bear to be parted from you.'

She smiled back into his eyes, wanting to drown herself in those blue pools. 'Yes, I'll come with you, Mike,' she said softly. 'I'll be with you always.'

Have a romantic Christmas.

Roses, Always Roses
CLAUDIA JAMESON

Lady Surrender
CAROLE MORTIMER

Malibu Music
ROSEMARY HAMMOND

The Other Side of Paradise
MARGARET PARGETER

Put some more romance into your Christmas, with four brand new titles from Mills and Boon in one attractive gift pack.

They're all perfect reading for the holiday, and at only £4.40 it's easy to give the gift of romance.

Or better still, drop a hint that you'd like a little romance this Christmas.

Available from 11th October 1985 – look out for this gift pack where you buy Mills and Boon.

The Rose of Romance

Mills & Boon

4 Doctor Nurse Romances
FREE

Coping with the daily tragedies and ordeals of a busy hospital, and sharing the satisfaction of a difficult job well done, people find themselves unexpectedly drawn together. Mills & Boon Doctor Nurse Romances capture perfectly the excitement, the intrigue and the emotions of modern medicine, that so often lead to overwhelming and blissful love. By becoming a regular reader of Mills & Boon Doctor Nurse Romances you can enjoy SIX superb new titles every two months plus a whole range of special benefits: your very own personal membership card, a free newsletter packed with recipes, competitions, bargain book offers, plus big cash savings.

**AND an Introductory FREE GIFT for YOU.
Turn over the page for details.**

**Fill in and send this coupon back today
and we'll send you**
4 Introductory
Doctor Nurse Romances yours to keep
FREE

At the same time we will reserve a
subscription to Mills & Boon
Doctor Nurse Romances for you. Every
two months you will receive the latest
6 new titles, delivered direct to your door.
You don't pay extra for delivery. Postage and
packing is always completely Free.
There is no obligation or commitment –
you receive books only for
as long as you want to.

**It's easy! Fill in the coupon below and return it to
MILLS & BOON READER SERVICE, FREEPOST, P.O. BOX 236,
CROYDON, SURREY CR9 9EL.**

**Please note: READERS IN SOUTH AFRICA write to
Mills & Boon Ltd., Postbag X3010,
Randburg 2125, S. Africa.**

- -